CLOISTERED

A flash fiction collection

LIZ KELLEBREW

Unsolicited Press
Portland, Oregon
www.unsolicitedpress.com
info@unsolicitedpress.com
619-354-8005

CLOISTERED
Copyright © 2026 Liz Kellebrew
All Rights Reserved.
Printed in the United States of America.
First Edition.
ISBN: 978-1-963115-92-5

This is a work of fiction. Any resemblance to actual people, living or dead, is pure coincidence—or just your imagination running wild. If you think you see yourself in these pages, congrats, but nope… not you.

All rights are reserved. That means no part of this book may be reproduced, copied, shared, screen-grabbed, tattooed, or otherwise distributed without written permission from the publisher. Translation: don't steal our words. If you love this book, buy it, gift it, rave about it to strangers—just don't pirate it.

Now that the legal stuff is out of the way, go ahead and dive in.

Distributed by Asterism Books
https://asterismbooks.com/

For wholesale orders:
Asterism Books
568 1st Avenue South, Ste 120
Seattle, WA 98104
(206) 485-4829
info@asterismbooks.com

Cover Design: Kathryn Gerhardt
Editor: Summer Stewart

CONTENTS

HUNT	13
CHERRY	16
EGG	19
SCRAPE	24
SKYDIVER	28
BANG	37
BOLT	40
BAYSIDE	43
CHOP	47
CLOISTERED	50
PLUNGE	54
DIME	58
BITE	61
BEETLE	65
FLAY	68
WRECK	70
BURST	73
MACH 3	76
TALON	79
SNARE	83
STRIPPED	85

SPIT	88
TREPANATION	91
AXE	94
QUARK	98
EBB	102
SHARD	106
SIMULATION, PART 1	109
SIMULATION, PART 2	112
WHOLE	115
SNAP	118
GALILEO	124
STORM	126
SCALPEL	130
HARBOR	132
BURN	134
HONEY	138
SWARM	142
LOCK	144
JACKED	147
COYOTE	150
ORBIT	154
PLANK	157
AXIS	159
RUMBLE	162

GRAVITY	166
HARVEST	168
LEVIATHAN	169
THRUST	171
RESISTANCE	173
DIVE	174
STREET OF CRANES	175
BOIL	177
SWELL	179
BUTTER, SHOT	181

CLOISTERED

Does the wolf in the iron cage run day and night in its narrow world?

Can Xue, *Dialogues in Paradise*

HUNT

The man in the house nicks his smooth brown thigh with a razor blade. Snap, the blood pops out. Bright red at first, turning green in the oxygen.

From the slit in his thigh, a tiger is born. It comes out whiskers first, smooth black nose, hot white fangs. It claws at his flesh, hind legs scrabbling for purchase on his femur, a deep ache a tearing a kick in his groin and then with a roar the tiger emerges, dripping green, leaps onto the floor and the wound on his thigh is still throbbing and wet but the adrenaline heat of relief dams up in his body like an ocean and he is amazed.

The tiger laps the blood off its fur, licks its chops. Purrs. It is the size of a cub, but it is no cub. It is a full-grown miniature Bengal tiger.

He forgets to pour alcohol on his cut, forgets the bandage, forgets the thrill. He feels lightheaded. He sees the gunslinger waiting on the other side of the window blinds, sees polished gun metal through the slats, and the tiger in here.

The air conditioner emits a fragrance of cotton candy. The cabinet television strokes its antenna, turns itself on. The tiger walks into the TV screen, onto a racetrack, and jumps on the backs of horses. Jockeys and thoroughbreds scream. There is a tumult of whips and hooves, but the tiger is unstoppable. He is a killing machine.

The man in the house changes the channel.

A Navajo medicine woman scatters pollen to the four directions. She plucks the legs off butterflies, braids them into her daughter's hair.

The daughter is to be married to an important chieftain. The two women will have a hogan of their own, a place where the sun falls in the winter and the shade cools in the summer.

Their wedding is at a monster truck rally. There is a demolition derby held in the couple's honor, a money dance, white dresses and halibut shipped overnight from Alaska.

The bed in their hogan is covered with bearskins. At night they wear the bearskins and go into the mountains to drink Icehouse in the forest. They find small men living in holes under tree roots. The men tell them they are living in sin. The women laugh and pluck off their limbs, one by one, until only their heads are left.

They eat the heads and spit out the teeth like blackberry seeds.

The man in the house changes the channel.

The owner of a taco truck adopts the tiger. He sleeps behind the warm stove all day and hunts for meat at night. Every morning, the owner makes tacos out of the leftover meat. They make a good team. The killer needs a good provider. He needs a place to dream.

One day a guru comes to the truck and buys dos tacos de papa, por favor. He drinks Sidral Mundet sitting in the shade of his unwound turban and tells the tiger he can teach him to become enlightened. No more killing, only peace.

The tiger likes this man. He likes the way he pulls at his fuzzy gray beard, the way he doesn't eat the tiger's carne asada. The tiger follows the guru into the desert to learn yoga, which he masters within a day. (Tigers are very flexible.) Then he learns levitation and firewalking by the end of the week. When the guru admits he has nothing left to teach him, the tiger is so hungry he almost kills and eats the guru, but he kills a jackal and eats its tough flesh instead.

The guru weeps. "And now it is I who should be learning from you," he says, "for the tiger has so mastered his own desire that now he can even kill without wanting to do so in the slightest."

The tiger cuts its forepaw with a claw. Snap, the blood pops out. The guru, still sobbing, crawls in. His bones crackle and pop as he is subsumed into the tiger's flesh. The guru's world tastes of metal, sublimely warm. It is dark as the womb.

When he is reborn, the guru is dressed in black. It is hot out here by this window. He is holding a gun.

He hears a television blaring inside. Horses roar and scream.

The man in the house changes the channel. Green blood drips down his leg.

CHERRY

Her nipples were small and soft in my mouth. "Are you getting any milk?" she asked.

"Yes," I lied, because I didn't want to hurt her feelings. We were playing mother and baby in the closet. Her brother, the buccaneer, kept watch from the bed.

"Mom's coming," he said. We came out and he went back to gluing his model airplane together, cursing his clumsy hook hand. He was always doing something with glue or soldering irons.

After dinner we walked across the field to the railroad tracks. The grass came up to my chest. Crickets sang and grasshoppers leapt away from our feet. When we could hear the rumble of the coming train, the buccaneer put a penny on the track.

"That's dangerous," my friend said. Her brother laughed.

We lay on our stomachs in the tall grass and felt the train coming in our guts, shaking up hamburger patties and green beans and Kraft Mac and Cheese into something big and terrible.

The train was loud like a universe exploding. The steel tracks bent under its weight. When the locomotive ran over the penny, it sparked and shot out like a hot bullet.

"Land ho!" her brother shouted, scrabbling for the penny in the weeds. I couldn't move. I was paralyzed, mesmerized by the power of the train. It moved so fast its wheels blurred, stretched so tall I couldn't see the top. One big black force blocking out the sky.

Then the red caboose, then the thunder eased. We brushed the dust off our knees. Her brother held up the flattened penny. We touched it. It was still hot.

"Put it in your mouth," he said, "but don't swallow it."

My friend's eyes were wide. I obeyed. The copper tasted electric on my tongue, like the time I plugged Mom's scissors into the power outlet. The world changed. The sky and the grass fell away, breaking up into tiny boxes. My friend and her brother fell apart into letters and numbers that bounced and rolled. I was floating in a dark sky like in Star Trek. There was nobody here, but there was everything else.

I was in trouble. I must have swallowed the penny. I tried to move but there was nowhere to go in space. Everything was so far away, and I didn't know which star was my sun.

A steaming cauldron appeared before me, and suddenly I wanted to put my foot in it. I took off my left foot, shoe and all, and put it in the pot.

I started stirring the pot. Beautiful music came from it, music so beautiful I could have cried. The stars echoed the sounds. I put my right foot in the pot, too.

Then I saw the tree of my life stretched out like a map below me. Everything behind me was one straight line. Everything before me was branches, as many branches as there were stars in the sky.

I looked closely at one of the branches and saw myself, an ant, an adult. I saw adult me pop a pimple on her face and a hundred thousand lives leaked out. I saw her take a shower with a strange man. I saw her squeezing avocadoes at the grocery store.

The branch went on like this for some time before it broke off the tree completely. A raven landed in the tree and plucked a cherry from it. The raven's eye was in the cherry.

I understood in my heart that the cherry seed was the seed that grew the whole universe. I wanted to eat that cherry more than anything.

Without my feet to hold me down, I found out I could fly. I followed the raven past comets and asteroid belts. I followed it through galaxies teeming like seas. I followed it through starfire.

It landed in the pine tree in my mother's backyard. It swallowed the cherry whole. The wind in the branches made the most beautiful music.

EGG

She cracked open an egg, and an eyeball fell into the hot skillet. It sizzled and flopped around until it found its way out, rolling off the stove and under the kitchen table.

It glared up at her through the layer of lint and toast crumbs it had accumulated. She got the broom and dustpan to sweep it up, but the eyeball didn't want to be touched. It kept bouncing out of reach. She decided it was best to leave it alone. She made oatmeal for breakfast instead. Her appetite for eggs was ruined.

There was a knock on the door. It was two very nice Mormon brothers selling cosmetics for their mother. She was in the hospital for a ruptured spleen.

As she flipped through the catalog trying to decide on a shade of lipstick, one of the boys took a tuba out of his pocket and played the national anthem. The other boy stood with the Book of Mormon over his heart. The cat came out to see what was happening but quickly walked away, tail twitching in disdain.

She chose Peach Summer for the lipstick. The boy with the tuba said he had brought some peyote and would she like to try some? She was about to politely decline when the other boy said, "Hey, is that an eyeball under your table?"

No sooner had he opened his mouth than the eyeball leapt right into it. He coughed and gasped, grabbed his head, stomped his feet. Bent over and tried to spit. His face contorted and his eyes bulged.

Suddenly, his right eye popped out, and there was the egg eye in its place.

The boy with the tuba put the peyote away. The cat slunk off with the boy's eye, but no one noticed. It was time for the presidential rally and the boys had to go, but the woman stayed home on account of her bad knee.

She threw the rest of her eggs in the trash and took it out to the curb.

At the rally, the boy with the tuba took off to play with a marauding troupe of Patriot Boys, but the boy with the eye didn't care. He had the eye now, and it knew things he didn't. it knew the president practiced cunnilingus with a Filet-O-Fish. It knew that the salesgirl at the Christian bookstore wore a necklace of her own baby teeth under her blouse. It knew that seagulls dreamed of being dragons, and that last year ten houseless people had fallen asleep in dumpsters and were never seen again.

The eye knew things he didn't want to know. He wanted to gouge it out. But he didn't know where his own eye had gone and he was also afraid of hurting himself, so he closed that eye instead. Then he walked through a cloud of tear gas and couldn't see anything.

The eye led him into a building that was forty stories high and full of water. The entrance doors suctioned closed behind him and the water in the lobby buoyed him up until he was level with the receptionist at the front desk.

"Here, put these on," she said.

The boy put on a pair of artificial gills, some goggles, and a visitor badge. He scanned the badge at the turnstile and was sucked up a tube of water to the elevator banks. There were dozens of people swimming around in their business casual skirts and blazers and slacks and ties, shooting up and down the elevator tubes. Bubbles came out of their mouths when they spoke.

In the cafeteria, people tilted their heads back and opened their mouths to catch the food that floated down from the ceiling. Once in a while a live fish would dart by, and there would be a friendly competition to see who would catch the fish first and get to eat sushi. Sometimes there would be a goat or a cow. These you had to grab by the feet and drag down. There would be a cloud of blood and then, whoosh! Everyone had steak tartare.

The water filters worked very well.

After lunch, the boy with the eye went to the top floor where a man in a white suit offered him a job. The man in the white suit had an office that sat in a glass dome of water on top of the building. You could almost see the mountains on the other side of the freeway, and the protestors at the presidential rally. You could definitely see all the other office buildings.

The boy accepted the job. It was a job wiping computers. He had to delete all the files from the computers of departed employees and sometimes he had to punch holes in hard drives. He liked the job because he could do it, and also no one ever commented on his weird eye.

One day he left work and forgot to take off his artificial gills. Outside, he gasped and spasmed on the hot sidewalk, feeling his flesh fry. A woman wearing neon pink pants bent over him.

"I remember you," she said. "You have my egg eye."

He coughed and tried to speak, but he couldn't breathe. The woman pulled at his gills, but they were stuck on tight.

"Help me," she called, but people kept passing her by.

The boy wasn't heavy, nor was he light. His hearing dimmed first, and then he couldn't see. But the eye could. The eye could see everything. The eye saw dung beetles rolling shit up trees. The eye saw a supernova with a toaster pastry in it. The eye saw God eating the toaster pastry. Crumbs and icing flecked his beard. The eye saw a man repairing a bidet in Japan. The bidet played music whenever it sprinkled. The eye saw a man in black removing the boy's gills, tilting his head back, placing his mouth over his (a gesture the boy would once have thought of as a sin), and as he gazed down lovingly at himself the woman in the neon pink pants said she never did get her Peach Summer lipstick.

The boy died, but the eye lived. The woman kept it in a jar in her kitchen and sang to it when she chopped garlic.

Five years later, the boy's brother got tired of playing tuba with the Patriot Boys. He found himself a good fat wife and married her under the St. Johns Bridge.

SCRAPE

The garter snake's slender belly bulged as it wound its pinstriped body into the blackberry vines at the edge of the sidewalk. Its bulge was the exact size and shape of a newborn mouse. Its tail was white and tapered at the end. Either it was shedding its skin, or someone had just run over it with a bicycle tire.

The snake stopped in the shade and raised its head. It had very good hearing. It heard the man in front of the grocery store beating a rhythm on his milk crate stool, asking for a dollar. It heard the teenage girl at the fast-food franchise crying in the bathroom. It heard the kids at the skate park crashing and swearing. It heard a widowed woman playing her piano scales. It heard mosquitoes buzz and church bells ring.

It heard the roots beneath the earth, growing.

Behind the blackberry hedge, a hungry man opened his mouth and waited for food to fall into it. He didn't care what, so long as it was edible. Statistically speaking, if he lay here in one spot like this, it was bound to happen sooner or later.

He lay on the open earth between two firs and a cedar and waited.

The snake gave birth to a human fetus. It was small as a newborn mouse and transparent pink. It had huge purple blobs where its eyes would be when they opened. It had no concept of gender or love. Everything was new.

The snake coiled itself around the fetus to keep it warm.

At the creek, a teenaged girl caught a rainbow trout. She bashed it on the head. It went still.

On the road, a real estate agent drove past the grade school. Her rear passenger tire turned into a Napoleonic soldier and rolled into the gutter.

The soldier untangled his bicorne hat from the plate-sized leaves of a vine maple. He almost stepped on the snake.

When he saw the naked human fetus, his throat filled with tenderness. He scooped it up and put it under his hat, feeling very paternal.

The snake slunk under the blackberry hedge and curled up on the chest of the hungry man. The hungry man had fallen asleep in the sun. His mouth was still open.

The man didn't dream, but the snake did.

A bored housewife whittled red alder on her front porch. Her knife was dull, but her teeth were sharp. The wood was red like blood where she cut it, red like her own blood from the nicks on her fingertips that stung and ached with raw new blisters as she fought to understand the grain.

The wood used to be a piece of tree. It remembered what it was like to be alive. It didn't want to be cut in places it once knew as body. Didn't want to be sliced against the inner vein.

The housewife was carving a fork. A fork to stab in a roast. A fork to flake a fish. A fork to spear a tender stem of broccolini, to shovel salad, to hold a juicy chicken breast in place while she sliced it.

Her husband called for his steak and potato but she didn't answer. She rubbed her forehead, smearing blood. Alder shavings flecked her hair. Sawdust clung to her boots. She was formidable.

"Why don't you answer when I call you?" her husband growled.

Zip! She cut off her tongue and threw it at his feet. It writhed and flopped like a living thing, curling like her husband's upper lip.

She smiled under his glare. The spaces between her sharp teeth filled with blood. The dog ran off with her tongue, and that was that. She never had to speak to her husband again.

The hungry man woke up. Some strange and delicious meat had fallen into his mouth. It was tender and chewy. The snake had given birth again.

The snake was tired of men stealing her children. She couldn't kill him, but she would make him cry. She bit the man's neck, hard. He screamed and throttled the snake to death.

It was a long death. A good one. The snake could hear everything. The scrape of knife on alder wood. The boots of soldier on the road. A half-wild dog feasting on tongue. A girl gutting a fish. A tow truck beeping. The acid in the man's belly, dissolving her child's flesh. The seedling heart of a human fetus, flopping, grating.

SKYDIVER

Crouched on the floor in the cabin of the Cessna, I braced myself against the wooden back of the pilot's seat. I was about to place my life in peril, testing my endurance and my wits yet again.

I checked my harness and watched the clouds slip by through the porthole window as the pilot flew me up. Ice formed on the Cessna's wings, which was dangerous, but once we cleared the clouds we'd see the sun and then I would jump, which was dangerous as well.

Any number of things could go wrong. The parachute might fail to open, the straps might break, I might forget to pull the chute at the proper altitude, or my altimeter could fog over. I'd prepared for all of these contingencies with countless hours of training and forty-two jumps under my belt, but anything was possible.

I told myself that all would be well. My nerves served merely to indicate my level of excitement regarding the jump. I was eager to dive into the troposphere once again, an atomic bundle of electron joy screaming triumph all through a 40-second freefall.

The cabin air grew chill, sun glared gray through wet clouds, and the ancient plane creaked and popped as its wood and steel contracted. My lungs expanded with each deepening breath.

I tightened my bootlaces and rechecked my straps. I flexed my fingers inside my gloves, ready for the door release, pitted by the grip of a thousand hands. Almost time to jump.

My harness felt too tight. This was good. This meant I wouldn't fall out of it in midair and smash into the ground at 125 miles an hour. I took a deep breath and visualized myself jumping, freefalling, pulling the rip cord, gliding into the hayfield behind the airport where my friends would be waiting for me, beers in hand.

But suddenly, something clanked and I heard a grinding noise as red light glared from the cockpit and the plane lurched to the left. I wedged myself into the corner between the wall and the back of the pilot's seat.

"Well, look at that," the pilot remarked, nonchalance in denim coveralls. "The engine's failing."

It was true. The plane shuddered, tilting so I'd have to climb up to the exit door.

I told myself not to panic, but I considered what might happen if the plane blew into pieces. We would crash and burn, leaving only our sooty skeletons to commemorate a 100-octane holocaust.

Red spots obscured the clear plastic of my altimeter gauge, but I wasn't bleeding, so I wiped the gauge on my pants. At

14,000 feet I'd be jumping 1,000 feet higher than usual, but it wouldn't make much difference.

"I can jump now," I shouted, pulling myself up toward the door.

The pilot let out a laugh that made my neck prickle. "I don't have a chute."

"I have one. I have a chute," I yelled. For fuck's sake, the man was crying. It really would be up to me to save us both.

I checked my altimeter again. The red needle kept sliding down. We'd have to jump soon. I didn't have a harness for the pilot, which complicated matters, but I could make it work. I'm a skydiver after all. That's what we do.

Then, the unthinkable. Something loosened from the propeller area and the plane thunked and stalled, shrapnel tearing off a chunk of wing. The plane rolled belly up, knocking me against its ceiling. My skull whacked against metal, I saw stars inside my eyelids, I'd bruised my spine, and if we stayed on that plane one moment longer we were both going to die. So I gripped the pilot's seatback with one hand, and with the other I helped him undo his safety belt. He was disoriented, so I grabbed him by the arm and pulled his heavy body with me toward the door. His breath thickened into choking gasps.

This was my forty-third jump, and I would live to make my forty-fourth. I could do this. I sat the pilot on my lap facing me. Our noses nearly touched.

"Hold on and don't let go," I instructed, and the pilot wrapped his thin limbs around me. I opened the door and inched my legs over the lip, grabbed the handles inside the doorway, and watched the clouds smoke underfoot. I rocked and counted to three before pushing out of the doomed aircraft just as my altimeter hit 13,000 feet.

Sweet freedom! We would live! The air rushed from my lungs and ice formed at the inside corners of my goggles, blue sky shimmered above us, and I forced out a roar so my lungs would have no choice but to inhale. And soon, it wouldn't be long, soon we would fall through the clouds and see the good green and brown squares of the forgiving earth below our swinging shoes.

"Get ready for this!" I laughed, ecstatic. But the pilot buried his face in my shoulder and said nothing, and I realized he was facing the wrong way. He wouldn't see the beauty of the earth, just the cold gray clouds and ice blue sky, and he clung to my ribs with a tightness like long-held breath.

Having cleared the ill-fated Cessna, I thought to find the pull handle for the parachute cord. My gloved hand came away from the pilot's back covered in blood. There was a dark, sopping gash in his coveralls that descended into flesh, puncturing deep striations of muscle and fat. I felt a sympathetic sting in my own chest.

The pilot turned his ashen face to reveal his right cheek smeared with blood as well. "You're hurt," he observed.

"You're in shock," I returned, but then I looked down and saw an identical wound just below my own left collarbone, and I shifted my shoulder to test the damage until a deep burning sensation stopped me. I couldn't believe I'd been so careless.

The pilot depended on me, and no matter how much blood I lost, I had to get him to safety.

"Hold on!" I shouted. I'd pull the rip cords once we'd descended to the correct altitude. Any sooner than 5,000 feet, and we stood a good chance of getting caught in an updraft and sailing out for miles before we could land. Overexposure to the freezing temperatures of the troposphere could kill us just as surely as a failed chute deployment.

I looked for the altimeter I'd strapped to my left hand, but it was gone. Not on my right hand, either, not on me at all, and the white dial on which our lives depended must even now be rattling around in the carcass of the plane, or dropping like a stone to earth, or slipping deep into the slick salt burgundy of the pilot's chest wound, burrowing a relentless tunnel toward the muscle and thrum of his heart.

Dirty clouds dampened our hair and our faces. Still, we fell. It was like falling through the smog which once plumed from the smokestacks of paper mills at the edge of the mint fields across the street from my mother's house. Powdered sulfur spotted the hood of her Chevy LUV pickup with poisoned pollen when the dew came, and there was cold gray metal beneath that paint for the whole world to see. My mother died in the spring when the daffodils had not quite opened, their yellow centers contained in the explosion of diesel and fire that burned her bones beneath the crunch of a flipped log truck.

If I had been there, I could have helped her get out before the fuel ignited. But I was in Vegas. Freefall convention.

I grasped for the chute's pull cord. Even if I pulled too soon, even if we did find an updraft and spiral for hours or days, it would be better than the certainty of snapped spines and splattered brains that would come if we dove headfirst into *terra firma*.

But the pull cord wasn't there. The toggle had dematerialized entirely, not even a loop of cord to hold on to, and I felt the gorge rising from my stomach for the first time since my seventh jump, when I'd forgotten to look at the altimeter and pulled the cord too late and broke both my ankles when I landed in a thicket of blackberry bushes as tall as a Humvee.

But the broken bones and the hundred thorns in my flesh would be nothing compared to the finality that awaited us if my chute did not deploy at all. How long had we been falling? How many thousands of linear feet separated our stick figure bodies from the bedrock of earth? How many square feet of air would we part like the Red Sea before we reached dry land?

How long would those final few seconds be?

Still we fell, silent and heavy as twin meteoroids, and we rushed closer and closer to the ground and I knew I couldn't let us die.

I balled my hands, cursing myself and my shortsightedness. Why hadn't I paid attention? I'd jumped forty-two times and I knew to check all my equipment before the jump. It just had to happen this one time, the time the plane failed, the time I failed.

I tilted my head back so the wind would pull the tears from my eyes. We were both dead now. I shouldn't have made him jump, because he might have had a chance. Maybe he could have landed the plane in the river somehow, or even the trees. Maybe he would have lived.

The hot breath of the pilot stirred in my ear. "Here, take it," he said. Tapping my hand, he pushed the hard sticky plastic of the pull cord toggles into my palms.

I wanted to scream, I wanted to swear at him. The pilot had quite possibly killed us both. But then again, perhaps he'd saved us instead, and besides there was no time for blame so I pulled the cord and tensed as I listened for the whip-slap sound of the chute unfurling and I bent my elbows, I raised my forearms and I urged the pilot to tighten his grip as we braced for the impact of the harness straps yanking into my flesh and jolting us to half our speed when the chute caught air. We would glide like loving seraphim over the glinting silver of necklace rivers, over green shag trees and brown acres of tilled loam, dangling our feet over microbial automobiles sliding in slow motion toward their dreamless destinations.

But there was nothing. No impact, no rush-whistle whip-slap yank of nylon, and the cord was as useless as my rage as the planet widened its hard horizons and the pilot's mouth widened in what could have been a scream of pain but I could not hear it for the roar of the wind. I pulled as hard as I could on the parachute cord and it finally snapped open and then we spiraled downward, which should not have happened, but as the sky and the earth changed places I realized the pilot's left arm had tangled in the rip cords and now the parachute was only halfway open. We would still die, and now I had even less control than I'd had during the freefall.

A sweep of fine snowflakes blasted my face as centripetal force jerked us like kites in a windstorm. I'd never had a son. We would never build a snowman together or jump in tandem from an airplane at 13,000 feet. I hadn't done anything to be remembered for, and maybe that was a blessing. I let the wind take my arms out, no longer caring whether the pilot could hold on to me with his own strength. It would be less painful for him if he let go of me now, but I no longer had the heart for honesty. I just didn't want to die alone.

Suddenly, the parachute cords snapped straight out and the canopy opened taut above us. The thick weight of the pilot anchored my middle as we braked, and in my relief I buried my face into his neck, telling him *sorry*, telling him *almost there*.

But the joy, I've never known such joy as when the clouds and snow finally broke and the ground opened up beneath us and it was everything I knew it would be and now there was the landing, the sweet fucking landing. I, Leo, could do this.

I pulled down steady on the chute handles and slowed our descent, suspending us under the milky murk of the sky. We hovered there between earth and air, reciprocating heartbeats, our flesh for flesh. And in that moment I was digested, and I passed through the bowels of a tiger, and a tree grew from the compost of my heart. But that tree was crooked and defiant, and refused to put down its roots. So we would fly, the pilot and I.

I let go of the toggles, and an updraft came just like I knew it would, and we flew on cold feathers above the altostratus and into the cirri. Icicles formed on our mustaches.

Still, we rose. We blew with the wind for a long while. Once, I woke up, and at that time I saw a rainbow of ice around the moon.

BANG

The cemetery road was muddy and steep. The city didn't have the money to maintain it, which was probably a good thing. If it weren't for the ruts, your car might slide right off and roll down the hill into the brush.

At the top, there was nothing but headstones and trees. Loose beer cans and wilted bouquets. A great-uncle's ashes were buried up here. Some kids who drowned in the river. At night you could sit with your back against a cedar and watch satellites track across stars. Afternoons, lay your head on the graves and feel how warm the earth was made by the sun. You could almost feel alive here, this place where everyone was dead.

Before you got here, you had to cross the freeway and the railroad tracks. Before that, two auto parts stores and a tavern. Before that, the market and the pharmacy. Before home, the river. Before the river, nothing. Everything.

The river was how you knew where you were going.

Strange things came out of the river, things that should not have been there. Whale bones and ostrich eggs, biker jackets and table legs. Movie projectors, gramophones, and file cabinets all bubbled out of the river at high tide and clung to the banks.

The Komodo dragons were the worst. They swarmed out of the river once a month and ate the neighborhood cats. The pharmacist stocked extra Xanax for the elderly women when the dragons were due. The gun shop owner sold more ammo to the men. There was a run on candy and soda at the grocery store because the kids wanted to stay up late and watch their dads blow the heads off dragons. Their fathers were dragon slayers. They were heroes.

Their mothers wore floral print sweatshirts and ate ranch dip out of Tupperware. They called each other on the phone and talked about everything but the dragons. It wasn't a nice thing to talk about, blowing the heads off lizards, or lizards eating people's cats. They let the men handle it. Killing was a man's job.

Their daughters washed the supper dishes until their hands sloughed off. Their hands went down the drain and into the river, which attracted more Komodo dragons. It was a vicious cycle.

The sons kept drinking milk. They drank until they vomited. There was nothing else to do.

At the lodge built of old growth timbers, the trees had shifted even in death. The stairs went up and down and sideways all in one flight. The lodge served elk and lizard burgers. Tourists and geologists came to worship at the mountain. They bought vials of sand to leave at the shrines where the trees had died. Late at night, there were bootleg tacos bought for a dollar off some kid's Coleman grill. They stuttered drunk on the Escher stairs and took a drink every time Queen Cersei fucked her brother.

That was a lot of drinking. When they went to bed it was almost dawn but the sun had never set. They sweat bullets in the attic with one window. Listened to an entire DMX album at full blast. Shed their skins and tried to snare moose in their rolls of belly fat.

The next morning, there was a string of dead daughters hanging from the lodge. Someone's dad had killed them all, shot them right in the head. Bang, the sun dropped to the porch floor. Trees whimpered. A ship tore itself in two and spilled ice into the river.

They built a castle with the ice, filled it with people and furs. Frogs jumped out of the elders' mouths, singing stories of famine and lust.

The old women died there, souls passing into vapor. Icicles crowning their fur.

The men all died young. Bang, they said. Boom, went the sun.

BOLT

She knew how to roll with the punches. Water high, barrel low. She bellied up and rumbled down. Ate spark plugs for breakfast and spit out the tips. She liked the sound they made on the garage floor. *Tang*, a sound you could taste with your tongue.

She didn't like people who minced their words. Didn't like cats. Didn't like dogs. She kept a tarantula in a fish tank and fed it thunder. She drank behind the wheel because she was looking for danger. As hard as she tried, it never found her. She was bored stiff. She pulled fire alarms and peeled other people's hangnails. Tore down stop signs and sprayed graffiti on model homes.

She was an unstoppable force. But it all stopped when she met M. Jones.

M. Jones was one bad motherfucker. He'd been in jail twice for reasons no one knew, and they all valued their lives too much to ask.

He stood outside the bar smoking and so did she. They stood under the eaves because it was raining. It rained so hard the puddles were topped with exclamation points, and the drops on the roof sounded like BB guns. Her ears were cold and her feet were wet. They blew smoke and laughed.

"Did you know," he said, "you can plant a hundred apple seeds from the same tree and never get the same fruit twice?"

It was love that first night. M. Jones hung his American flag skullcap on the corner of her four-poster bed and they released the tarantula into the wild. She didn't need to hold it captive anymore.

It was love the second night. They went four-wheeling and she crashed her ATV into a tree.

On the third night, they drank Wild Turkey for dinner and bought rifles at Walmart. "Quit your job and come see the country with me," he said. So she climbed into the cab of his 18-wheeler and off they went.

They drove through lightning bolt monsoons in Tempe, saw Death Valley in the heat of the day. Rolled past moonlit sagebrush in Oregon, hauled over snow-white mountains in Washington State. It was maybe somewhat possibly actually love. She didn't want for anything. She wanted more. She was happy with him. She was terribly bored. She didn't want to be alone, but she missed the taste of danger more.

She felt like a forest fire, devouring all in her path. The truck cab was a cage, she was trapped, so she escaped. She ran into the desert, sand stinging her legs. The hair on her arms stood on end.

The moon rose among cacti. She felt she could see it in eight dimensions, so vivid was her sight. She wondered why all cacti grew up to look the same. And then the crickets chirped their eerie songs, so beautiful it made her eyes sting.

She cupped a cricket between her palms, popped it in her mouth. Chewed, swallowed, spit out the legs. She liked the crunch it made, a sound she could taste.

BAYSIDE

Raymond sat on a milk crate at the fruit stand, shaving his head. His cat watched flies buzz above the dragonfruit.

"Lazy cat," Raymond scolded, wiping lather off his razor with a rag. "Why don't you do something about those mice?"

The cat blinked, appalled by the man's blatant speciesism. She herself had no need to supplement her diet with mice when the butcher across the street fed her chicken livers and hearts each day. At least someone else's hands were dirty with those killings. She was comfortable with that. She wasn't going to let the organs of the dead go to waste.

A gray mouse popped out of a box with a kumquat in its mouth. Raymond swiped at it with his razor and missed.

He glared at the cat. "That was *your* job."

There was only so much one could take. The cat walked out of the fruit stand, tail held high.

At the waterfront, mermaids flashed their sharp yellow teeth and made deals with the longshoremen. Someone in an Elmo costume pounded their fists into the belly of someone in a dinosaur costume. The chocolatiers flashed edible iPad cases in milk, white, and dark chocolate. They even had designer artisanal cases for the (shh, don't tell anyone) new iPad prototype. A woman with hibiscus in her hair chiseled paint into bridges. A chef screamed something about birds in the Parmesan and jumped off the pier. A couple wearing matching tracksuits pushed their matching chihuahuas in a baby carriage. A trolley bell clanged.

The cat was terribly interested in the Parmesan birds, but they didn't seem to exist.

On the top floor of a flatiron building, a garment worker named Lin spun cottonwood fluff into thread. There were machines that could do this, but only humans could produce the organic, handspun, 100% vegan thread that was in such high demand these days. Next week, she would work the loom to weave the thread into artisanal cloth. The week after that she would sew the cloth with the thread into American-made, animal-safe, dry clean only button-up shirts to be sold at stores she was not allowed to name.

Lin made five dollars an hour. This was very good money back home. She slept on a cot in a room with twelve other people, not counting the two babies.

You got used to it. At least she had a job. On the days she worked the loom or spun the thread, she could gaze out the window at the city. There, in a thumb-sized gap between two skyscrapers, she could see the ocean. Some days it was blue, other days brown or green. On sunny days it flashed so bright it left a white rectangle in her eyes. Most days it was gray, gray as the sky.

She never went to the waterfront. She didn't have time. Every third weekend she got two days off, and she went to the library to teach herself how to read English.

Morris spent Saturdays at the library trying to pick up chicks. He hadn't had any luck so far, but this didn't stop him from trying. He liked photography books and atlases because they gave him ideas. His favorite person was the gray-haired librarian with the purple cat's-eye glasses. She always winked and gave him a sticker, even if he was a full-grown man.

Morris had Downs. He knew he was special. He wore a safety vest over his clothes and wore his bike helmet indoors. He had what his Mom called a very thick skin. He liked photography books about tigers and travel books about India.

The most important thing about Morris was that he never, ever gave up. He kept eating his single-serve bowls of gluten-free Rice Chex in the library, even though you weren't supposed to. He rode his bike ten miles each way to get there so he could improve his body as well as his mind. And he kept asking the girls in the computer area to go out with him. This was also against the rules, but most of the time they just ignored him, so he didn't see how it could be that bad.

One day he asked out a girl with orange hair and she told him he should try online dating. It was how she met her girlfriend, she said.

Leila programmed chat bots for human companionship. At night she watched *kaiju* films or read sci-fi novels and masturbated with the handle of a rubber spatula. She believed in exercising the clitoris just like any other muscle.

Although she made frequent use of her library card, she didn't like going outside. The people out there scared her. Once she'd ventured out for fish and chips and saw a guy in an Elmo costume beating the shit out of Barney the purple dinosaur for hanging out on his corner. She'd lived off teriyaki from the corner store ever since.

Abe had run the corner store for fifteen years, and he still worked 9-9 every day. He liked to talk to his customers when they came in to buy cigarettes and mini donuts. He asked them about their jobs and their families. He watched soccer on the TV behind the counter and sold chicken teriyaki made with meat from the local butcher. He sold bananas and apples that he bought at a discount from Raymond at the fruit stand.

When Raymond came in to buy his nightly burrito, he found an orange-haired girl feeding chicken to his cat.

"So this is why my cat never catches any mice," he said. "You know what? You can keep her."

Leila and the cat lived contentedly from then on.

CHOP

The waiting room was impossibly large, and had too few chairs. They had been waiting all this time only to find out they were already on the boat, and the boat was taking on water. The captain made an announcement. They went upstairs onto the deck. The sky was gray and the water was cold. It licked its chops at the edges of the sun deck.

Even colder than the water was the dread. It took her in its mouth from head to toe. Her heart stood still like a burrowed animal, her breath held hard like a jewel in her chest. The boat struggled. The harbor was near. Where was her beloved? The icy harbor was about to swallow them whole.

Two green helicopters rattled her teeth. They wore flags and rifles. They circled, attracted to death. They were locusts, not machines.

Below, the young men harvested the fields, naked to the waist. The spiders were trying to attract mates. That's what time of year it was. The young men pulled up radishes and flash grenades and beets. They wore zip ties on their wrists, pulled weeds out with their teeth. Their hands were as scarred as the face of the moon.

They filled baskets with dog bones, boxes with corn, bushels with eggplants and feathers. They dug and plucked with hands tied. They were told they needed to work, needed it like the loam needs rain. They were born to labor.

Their mothers labored, too. They sheared the hairs off fleas. They were paid by the pound. They ate oysters they grew in their bathtubs. They mowed the ancient mounds.

The mounds were built by who knows who. The mounds crawled with animals. You could put your ear up to them and hear the Milky Way, all static and squeaking. You could pierce your heart that way—the radio waves were that spiked. You could forget everything you'd ever learned about the tomb.

Then the summer, the snow of cottonwood seeds, and heat unbearable. She kept the cottonwood fluff in a jar on her desk because it pleased her. It was smooth as silk and held potential. You could grow a tree a hundred feet high from something the size of a sesame seed. She kept a down feather, too. It had come to her on a zephyr the eve of the heat wave, some sparrow's parting gift.

The archaeologists who found the jar centuries later would speculate as to its purposes. Were its contents used to apply cosmetics, pounded into medicines, eaten as food? Were the spiral shell and polished stones objects of worship? The objects were left in haste when the volcano erupted without warning on that hot and fatal day. All those bodies exposed to fiery ash, mud and lava flooding the valleys. The terroir of Jupiter in their hearts.

There were some who survived, fled to higher ground or set sail on the ocean. The rich men's bunkers underground were sealed in a tomb of rock. No one wants to know what they did when their food ran out.

Look, the raven comes bearing a fig leaf! Somewhere, there is food.

She knows that she is too far gone to make it. The raven knows, too. It lays down its head, a sacrifice. She cannot bear to take it, but she does.

She drinks its life, wears the feathers on her skin. She eats the meat and it pleases her. Strengthened, she walks on.

CLOISTERED

"Where are you from?" the border agent asked, analyzing her from behind his aviator sunglasses. He pinched her passport in his claws.

"The universe," she replied, then bit her lip. By his smirk she knew she'd erred.

The nurses in line behind her tittered. One carried a baby velociraptor wrapped in a white towel. The Virgin and Child.

Another nurse prepared a serum in a syringe. A vaccine against fear. "For the baby," she said.

She moved fast as a bolt of lightning, stole the syringe, and injected the border agent. His eyes lit up like sunsets behind the glasses. He laughed. Ordered the soldiers to take her away.

She had made another mistake. It had not been fear that caused the agent to stop her. Merely hate.

The fingers of the soldiers dug into her arms on either side. It hurt like hell. She asked them to stop. "You're hurting me."

"No, we're not," they said. "Be quiet, you."

"I'll tell the press. I'll tell the police."

"Who's gonna believe you?" they sneered. Their lips curled, showing teeth. Their hate was more than hate. It had grown up into full-fledged banality. They were just doing their jobs, and she was just another bag of meat.

They threw her in a cage with other women. They threw her hard so her head smacked the concrete floor. Lights glared. The door slammed. The back of her head felt warm and wet.

The women gathered around her. They dipped their fingers in the blood spilled from her head. They rubbed it on the sides and top of the cage door. They wanted no evil to enter.

"As long as we stay inside, we are safe," they told her.

A nurse came and shaved her head, stitched up her wound. There were bloody rags everywhere.

The mother in the corner kept crying for her baby, but no one knew where he was.

A cloud of monarch butterflies flew into the cage. They were thirsty, so the mother nursed them. Wings covered her breasts like armor.

There were perches and trapezes and mirrors in the cage. One corner was covered in newspaper. When she had to pee, she tried to read yesterday's news before the ink bled. She learned that a cryptocurrency mogul was running for president and a petroleum corporation shot a monster truck into space. That the ancient Israelites burned cannabis in their temples and that humans had been making fires for longer than anyone thought. That 30% of Americans would refuse the anti-fear vaccine because they were afraid of mind-controlling nanobots.

She wiped herself with an obituary and wondered why late-stage capitalism even needed nanobots. Wasn't addiction to consumption enough?

There was a trough in the corner that filled with amaranth seeds every morning. The women sucked them all day until they were soft enough to digest. They preened in front of the mirror, jostling for position, as if redder lips and thinner brows would buy their freedom.

One morning her stitches itched. She rubbed the back of her head and grabbed a handful of white worms. Horrified, she pulled out as many worms as she could find and threw them on the floor.

The worms began to eat the wire bars of the cage. The women were too busy preening to notice, even though she begged them to look.

There was a mighty whirlwind and out of it came a thousand thousand butterflies. They ate the cage, too. They ate until there was nothing left.

The weeping mother went out rejoicing.

There was a cool feeling, as though the top of her head had opened up like a treasure chest ready to receive all the mysteries of the world. She begged the others to come with her, but they were pecking like hens at the broken pieces of the mirror. The butterflies, sated, had flown away.

She followed the butterflies' lead.

As she left the place of cages, the soldiers and border agents gave chase. She kept walking. She refused to run. Her breath was a cloistered ocean in her chest. As she stepped into the desert, she fell into the stars. The soldiers fell, too. The border agent screamed. He must have been immune to the anti-fear serum.

The mouth of her head opened wide and swallowed the stars. It swallowed the men and their fear. Her brain burped, satisfied.

One big white worm emerged, the last one from the healed wound on her head. She cradled it like a baby as the galaxies spun by. It slept in a cocoon. It hatched with bright orange wings. It carried her all the way home.

PLUNGE

She chipped her tooth on a baguette. That's what she got for trying to eat French bread in the Netherlands.

Wisteria blooms hung like grapes over doorways set in red brick homes. Train tracks crossed the water. Everywhere there was water.

She took the tram to the coast and imagined Viking ships crossing the cold gray sea. Mondrian banners hung from power lines. Men kissed each other in front of the mosques. She couldn't cross the street on account of all the bicycles. She bought soppressata at Aldi and lived off chocolate and cheese. There were free oranges in the hotel lobby. At the Van Gogh Museum she thought she would feel most fulfilled to see *Vase with Twelve Sunflowers* and *The Starry Night*, but she was surprised to find that the painting that moved her the most was *Basket of Potatoes*. In the museum lighting, the thick ridges of paint gave each potato a silver lining.

She remembered digging in the dirt of her parents' cellar and how the brown soil would glitter with bits of ground-up glass from the old days when people buried their garbage next to their homes. Let worms and beetles do their work.

The antique collectors came to the house and asked to dig there. They found medicine bottles and liquor bottles. They auctioned them off for money. This was how they made their living.

They also sold encyclopedias. This was before the internet. She wondered what it had been like, to live with a knowledge that was fixed in time. Bound in the pages of a book. It explained why her parents were so set in their ways. They didn't know the truth was always changing.

It was worth it, to spend time in a place where she didn't know anything. Not like the place where she'd grown up, where she knew too much.

She remembered the Fourth of July back home at the lake. Invasive rodents from South America lived there. They grew to the size of small dogs and ate all the catfish in the lake. Then they came onto land and ate out of garbage cans, spilling garbage in the middle of the night, getting into spats with alley cats and raccoons. Bored middle-aged men threw hot crab legs off the grill to watch the animals fight while their wives helped their children with their algebra homework. Young people in their twenties who had just moved out of their parents' homes drank hard seltzer and shot Roman candles at each other in mock wars. There was cheap pizza and heavy petting later.

Church bells rang at six o' clock. No one was in church. The bells were automatic. All the preachers in town had the night off. They dressed like aunties and drank vodka out of lidded travel mugs.

A woman who had moved to the lake from Cambodia sold candy to feed her family. Each candy made you feel something different: happy, surprised, mad, ecstatic, in love, warm, tingly, lighter than air. You could eat all kinds at once and come out feeling perfectly calm. There was no candy that made you feel sad. Those were too hard to sell here, the woman said. No one would buy them.

When the fireworks began, it was pitch black and cold. People huddled together under blankets. The giant rodents huddled together near the blankets. The air filled with the stench of smoke. Flashing lights burned the backs of eyes. People said *ooh* and *aah*, as if pyrotechnics hadn't been invented a thousand years before. An aging hippie couple wearing matching tutus danced with sparklers and hula hoops.

A kraken rose up from the bottom of the lake, but no one noticed.

She had eaten the candy that made you feel happy, but instead of feeling happy, she found she was paying attention. She could see the kraken. She could see the curvature of the earth, how it rolled away from her slope-shouldered into darkness. She could feel a stranger's hand brush her butt cheeks through the thin fabric of her dress. She could smell the stale grease in the fryer of the food truck that sold elephant ears, hear the screams of earless elephants in India, their new silence a horror worse than death. She knew there were stars that she could not see. Oh, what of those stars! At the edge of the city by the paper mill, sulfur fell on the mint fields and brown cows pressed wet noses against a barbed wire fence, drawing blood.

She could stand in the middle of those fields and scream for hours and no one would come.

But the pitiless sodium lamps in the distance would light the river orange all night long, and the ships would come to take the bones of trees across the ocean, and her feet would sink into the marvelous mud of that marshland and down she would drown like a stone.

DIME

Instead of going to art school, Aurelia married a man who was still a boy and played video games all the time. She didn't like the way he made love, as though her body were an assemblage of buttons and joysticks that he could manipulate to achieve his expected goal.

The bridal shower had been hell. Her mother's church friends brought wrapped boxes of lingerie and Pyrex. She never used either, but the knife set she kept after the divorce. The blades stayed sharp even when she threw them into trees for target practice.

She had a black belt in Judo. She was broke. She lay awake nights listening to the neighbors scream at their children and waited for morning when she ate a spoonful of peanut butter for breakfast and bought a two-dollar mocha from the ExpressoRama drive-thru. The barista had a beak-shaped mouth and a third arm with suckers on it like a tentacle. She wore long sleeves but you could see the cup-shaped rims pressing up against the fabric of the shirt. She was always very polite.

At work, she started early. She worked at a pet store because she liked the smell of cedar shavings and bird seed. She cleaned the cages and aquariums first thing. The monkey flipped her off while she changed its diaper. He'd learned that from the customers. In revenge, she withheld his banana until mid-morning. She gave it to him when her first customers arrived, a young girl and her grandmother. They watched in fascination as the monkey simultaneously ate, screeched, and smacked the front of his diaper.

He reminded her of her ex.

The child asked her grandmother for a dime. They wore dark, old-fashioned clothing. She suspected the grandmother was something of a seamstress. You couldn't find kid's clothes like that at department stores.

The grandmother opened her red leather purse. It was big enough to hold a bowling ball. From among the packets of tissue and wrapped butterscotch candies she produced a smaller change purse.

The child put the dime into the vending machine full of generic brand M&Ms, but she struggled to turn the mechanical handle, and the grandmother's hands were too arthritic to get a good grip.

Aurelia volunteered to help, turning the handle with her wide strong hand. The candies clattered into the metal chute.

"Thank you," the child remembered to say, and cupped her hands beneath the chute. The grandmother lifted the metal door and the colorful discs fell into the child's hands.

The monkey shrieked with jealousy, which set the puppies barking.

"Can I see the puppies?" the child asked. Her hands were already empty, chocolate smearing her face.

"Sure, they're right this way." She led them down the aquarium aisle toward the window display and let herself in through the small bolted door meant to keep the pups from escaping.

The grandmother picked the child up so she could see the litter of golden retrievers frolicking in the sunlight.

Aurelia gave the child a tennis ball to throw for the puppies until the grandmother's arms grew tired and she set the child down.

The child began to cry, so Aurelia let her hold one of the pups. But the puppy shrank away, shivering.

"I wish we could keep him, Grandma," the girl said.

"There now, we'd better put it back." The grandmother patted the child's arm and she reluctantly let the puppy go.

The two of them left, the bell on the shop door ringing in their wake. Aurelia watched them meander down the sunny sidewalk. In the shadows of the shop awnings, their bodies flickered like images in a flip book. Eventually, they disappeared.

BITE

At high tea, she unwrapped the lacy pink box. Out popped a guinea pig with a flak jacket strapped to its chest. Its feces smelled like rotten hay. Its horrible beady eyes bulged. This was highly improper.

She'd never asked for a guinea pig. She didn't want one. This was the worst birthday ever.

The guinea pig ripped and scratched at her fingers. She yelped and dropped the box just as the white-gloved maitre'd appeared with the silver tea service. The guinea pig charged across the marble floor and barreled into the maitre'd's foot.

The maitre'd went down. All of her friends gasped as china teacups shattered and hot water flooded the floor. Individually wrapped tea bags lay scattered in the debris as if her horrible brother had started a game of 52-card pickup.

Fortunately, the petit fours on the table were still edible. She ate one with yellow icing and silver sugar pearls just as the guinea pig pulled a hand grenade out of its jacket pocket.

"For victory!" it cried, and pulled the pin.

She was closest to the window, so she got out first. As she stumbled through the rose bushes, shock shivering up her legs, the tea room exploded behind her. She couldn't hear. There was fire and smoke. Little bits of her friends' dresses floated down like snow: china blue from Jessica's puffed sleeve number, white lace from Becky's Victorian knockoff, floral bits from the Wallace sisters, neon green from stylish Shayna.

Shayna had almost made it. Her bloodied upper half hung from the windowsill like a Halloween decoration.

Fire trucks came, and an ambulance. She sank onto the grass by the roots of an ancient oak tree and picked up acorns. Her great uncle had made her an acorn person when she was five. It had a body of yellow cotton and two tiny acorn eyes, and a blue tam o' shanter with a stripe of tartan plaid.

Eight furry, jointed legs slipped out from the base of the tree and wrapped themselves around her. She was yanked down under the earth.

She yelled for help, but all she got was a mouthful of dirt. The spider must be enormous. It had already bit and paralyzed her. She would be dead soon. It would suck out her blood, use it to spin a web or lay eggs. But she was suddenly so sleepy, she didn't care.

She didn't expect to wake up, but she did. She had a pounding headache and couldn't see anything. She could hear things with many legs skittering around in the dark. She smelled the thick decay of deep earth, that smell after her grandpa rototilled the garden.

Someone asked if she was thirsty. As her eyes adjusted to the dark, she learned that the voice belonged to a young man only a few years older than she was. He was so handsome it made her whole body blush. He brought her a cup of cool nectar and she drank it down. It made her feel calm like the spider venom had, but without putting her to sleep.

He asked if it would please her to attend the festival with him. She said yes. She had no other thought but yes.

He led her down a tunnel toward a faint green light. He had phosphorescent wings and smelled of fresh-cut grass.

Everyone at the festival glowed: green, white, yellow, or blue. They had wings or antennae, compound eyes or mandibles, but underneath they were exquisitely human. Chain-smoking carneys ran amusement park rides. Children clutched their stomachs from too much cotton candy. Women with knee-length hair sold hand-carved lanterns and homegrown spices, while farmers sold nuts and mushrooms. There was a yoga class in progress.

They didn't walk through the animal barns because she was afraid of seeing a guinea pig. After they'd seen everything else, they left, walking against the flow of the incoming crowds. The air grew chill and her neck tingled. But the green glow of her companion's wings brought her comfort, so she followed him out into the darker cold.

They walked together for some time and then the ceiling opened up. Before her sprawled an underground ocean. The waves rolled in, glowing silver. She smelled sulfur instead of salt. Specks of mica glittered above them like stars.

The ocean was vast. Eyeless creatures swam and splashed in it. The icy water lapped at her bare toes.

Her companion squeezed her hand. She looked at her arm and saw it was fuzzy and blue. All of her was, even the skin beneath her dress. She knew she should be afraid but she wasn't. Whatever was growing on her gave off a gentle light and sprang up soft like moss. Slender pink mushrooms opened their umbrella heads in the crooks of her elbows and the nooks between her fingers.

The sightless fish flopped out of the ocean to kiss the fungi on her feet, and she knew that she was loved. Not loved like her parents loved, out of guilt and obligation. Not loved like her friends loved, for her possessions and curly hair. She was loved simply for existing, and the shock of that knowing folded her onto her knees.

The silver waves kept rolling. The sea slugs and eels kept kissing. Worshipping. Her companion cocooned her with his bright wings. All was still.

BEETLE

After the storm, the trees dripped. Doves hooted. Roof gutters sighed. Her tea had gone cold, the teabag wallowing in its depths like a waterlogged tampon.

Her phone rang, but no one was there. A robocall speaking perfect Mandarin. A slug stretched itself along the balcony. It was fat and brown and headed for a fallen crabapple. It was so slow it didn't even look like it was moving. Only its antennae waved, twisting east and then west.

She wound herself up in a sweater. She drank the cold tea. Her heart beat loudly from the willow tree outside, pounding like a jackhammer. It made her head hurt. She had to make it stop.

She'd cut out her heart a long time ago. It was too much maintenance. It made so much noise she couldn't think, so she put it in a jar in the crook of the willow tree and let mushrooms grow over it. The turkey tails were especially good this time of year.

She put on her boots and splashed out into the puddles. The sky glared like stainless steel. Her ankles were freezing. She couldn't find the jar with her heart in it at first. There was so much new growth. Fungus and lichens, small villages of ants and moss. Moldering leaves and a squirrel's stash of acorns. Still, her heart boomed like a machine gun.

Stop. Breathe. Calm. Her fingers brushed the chilled glass of the jar and something stabbed her in the palm. She swore and yanked her hand back. Blood bubbled up. Her flesh stung.

It was a beetle, and not just any beetle. A scarab beetle as big as the jar, with fearsome pincers. Black and so bright it hurt her eyes. She looked away.

Her heart started screaming. It was getting worse. She'd never be able to sleep tonight.

The beetle unscrewed the lid and crawled into the jar, where it suckled the heart. The heart fed quietly, content for the moment. But she knew it wouldn't last. No, cutting it out had not been enough. She would have to destroy it. It was the only way she could bear to live.

She screwed the lid back on and hurled the jar onto the pavement. The glass shattered, cutting the heart into a million pieces. The beetle lay speared through its soft belly.

A Steller's jay picked up the crabapple from the balcony. Thwarted in its mission, the slug fell to earth with a plop.

The earth broke open. The willow tree split. A shaft of lightning and a galaxy unfolded, swift as spilled milk. It opened her up, unpeeled the place in her chest where her heart used to be. Her head expanded, filling the emptiness of space. She was unbreakable, unstoppable. She knew where the end was. She was erupting and exploding and burning alive. And there, smoking in the shining plasma of new stars was her pulsar heart.

Oh, how she wanted to touch it. How she wanted to love it, this sun-white being of heat. It shuddered and skipped like a flame in the wind. It flashed like a lighthouse beam. It bared its strong teeth, its molten iron core. And when it sang, it scarred her, disfigured her soul, carved out her bones and scored her soft throat. She loved it she loved it she loved it and it would never love her back.

FLAY

He was slicing lamb chops off the rack because it was his job. The lady with the bright red mask wanted four value packs of lamb chops. That was forty. It wasn't even Easter.

A fly landed on his shoulder and began singing "*La donna è mobile*" in a lovely sonorous tenor. For its efforts, he gave it a scrap of marbled fat.

The fly was in heaven, which gave the man joy because flies have such short lives. As the fly feasted on the fat in the corner, he sold the lady her forty lamb chops. Forty pieces of silver flew out of her pockets and rolled around the butcher shop like leaves in the wind.

As he swept up the coins, his boss killed the fly with a rolled-up newspaper.

It hurt him like a gut punch.

The headline read, DEATH IN THE HARBOR. The broken body of the fly punctuated a photograph of a shipwreck. Its yellow innards trailed behind it like seasickness. The pink smear of lamb fat anointed the ship's shattered hull with blood.

The half-sliced rack of lamb dripped on the counter.

"No, no, no, you've been cutting it wrong," his boss said, grabbing the cleaver. "You must love the lamb, not hack at it. Love it like your child."

Clang. The cleaver hove the lamb. "Like this, see? One clean cut." Crack. "The bone falls away like butter, beautiful butter. Here, you try it."

As a child, the man had been asked to dedicate his life to God. Whack. The lamb was slain. His father said he loved him more than anything, which was why he sacrificed his only son to God. Slap. The tender lamb fell away like an opened book. Snap. The lamb was laid out on the counter, waiting to be consumed. In its short life, had it known love?

He knew the truth was dark and cages. The young sheep were raised merely to die, their sweet mild flesh a pleasing offering to the hordes.

The newspaper uncurled itself on the counter. In a postmortem reflex, the fly's leg twitched.

WRECK

After it collided with another ship, the cargo ship shat tons of merchandise into the harbor: nails and televisions and clothes. The Dungeness crabs sported bright blue polo shirts and whales wore magnificent skirts. A leviathan spent the better part of a day looking for a blazer that would fit, but he eventually left empty-finned and disappointed. It leaves a bad taste in your mouth when you can't find any clothes that fit.

Melanie knew. That's why she washed the taste away with beer after every foiled shopping trip. She hated the filtered air in the mall, laced with chemical dyes and artificially scented fruit lotions and the knife tang of heavy perfumes.

She hated the sales people with their perky names like Chase and Madison, hated their stick-thin limbs and Grand Canyon thigh gaps. Even the boys had them these days. She wondered whether their skinny jeans disguised Spanx made to flatten their balls. Wondered whether they were secretly smirking when she asked if they had a larger size in the back. For the record, the answer was always no.

She was drinking a second pint with her boyfriend on the patio at Ivar's by the harbor. A plastic package bubbled up in the water at their feet. She reached between the railing and snatched it up. Designer jeans, in her size!

"Bet those are covered in five kinds of crap," her boyfriend said, amused.

Melanie didn't care. They would wash.

As she suspected, the jeans fit perfectly. It was only after a month or so that things started to get strange.

She saw things that weren't there: medieval minstrels and sci-fi monsters, sharp-toothed octopod things, out of the corner of her eye.

She cut back on caffeine, but that didn't help. Her world shifted further—everything slanted at an angle. No more clean edges or straight lines.

She bought a new pair of glasses and stopped trying to see things that were far away. Then the men hawking their rap CDs on the street corner started to pay her compliments. A woman in a tie-dyed shirt hit on her. A man sitting in front of Caffe Vita told her she had a fine ass. The Tesla salesman, a six-foot-tall rat on his smoke break, gave her his number just because she walked by. Overwhelmed, she began to feel sick.

Her boyfriend loved the jeans, though. And she no longer had to endure the mockery of the anorexic salesboys. So she kept wearing the jeans, ignoring the hallucinations and harassment alike. She plastered a fierce don't-fuck-with-me look on her face and walked fast. She lost weight because she lost her appetite. She didn't enjoy drinking beer or going out to eat like she used to. She mostly stayed in, chugging unflavored seltzer and eating salads that made her shit.

One unholy day, the phantom minstrels wouldn't stop strumming their lyres and singing unintelligibly in Old English. She tried going down on her boyfriend, but the alien octopod shoved her out of the way and took over. Worse, her boyfriend didn't even notice.

Then the inside of her apartment broke apart and drifted around her like pieces of a Picasso painting. She had to get out. On the balcony, she took off her glasses. At the bus stop below, a man high on something yelled up at her that she had nice tits. Then he resumed shattering the tempered glass of the bus shelter with a metal pipe.

Melanie took off the perfect jeans and tossed them off the balcony. Her pale dimpled thighs got goosebumps from the wind. Her belly hung out above and below her panties, and her thighs rubbed together like a couple of dry-humping teenagers. She decided that all of this was fine.

Now that he was done breaking the bus shelter, the man dropped the metal pipe. It clattered onto the pavement as he picked up Melanie's jeans and whooped.

"Thanks, lady! I'm gonna sell these and buy me some crack!" The bus pulled up and he disappeared.

Melanie went inside. Her boyfriend snored on the couch. She went to the fridge and cracked open an ice-cold beer.

BURST

He was at the bus stop minding his own business when a person of short stature asked him for the time.

It was 12:05, he said. And he was headed out early even though the bars were still open. His shift was over and he wanted to get to the 24-hour QFC before the drunk rush. He had an urge to buy a slice of red velvet cake. Plus, he was out of scotch. And why the hell was the bus so late? Traffic was basically non-existent at this hour.

The short person nodded empathetically and pulled a long strand of seaweed out of his ear. He examined it and flicked it into the gutter. The bus pulled up and the seaweed clung to one of its tires.

All desire for cake suddenly drained out of him. The person of short stature boarded the bus, but he waved it on and went to the pinball arcade instead.

There, a live crocodile opened its jaws to accept hunks of raw poultry. He ordered scotch with MD and peed in a toilet that looked like the Batmobile. Androgynous blondes wearing glasses waited outside the all-gender restroom for him to emerge. He felt sweaty and gross. He drank three limoncellos and then walked up the hill toward his apartment.

He was halfway home when the earthquake hit. It shook open the pavement, cracked canyons down the streets. Apartment towers skidded downward. A woman in manacles burst out of the sewer, her eyes alight. She stretched like a cat and scraped the slime off her legs with the links of her handcuffs.

The ground was still rippling. The woman had no shoes, but she walked to the Pie Bar to quench her terrible thirst. She drank an entire pitcher of mimosas. She ate a huckleberry pie. The Pie Bar slid down the hill like melted ice cream and spit her into the bay where the saltwater rusted through her chains.

Free at last, she swam to the surface. There bobbing next to her was a man wearing a black hoodie and a look of confusion.

The man couldn't say what she saw in him. Getting thrown off the hill by an earthquake after a night of drinking hadn't done much for his looks. But she didn't seem to mind. They made out in the frigid waters, the incoming tide pushing them to shore. He thought of alien abductions. Maybe he was getting abducted right now.

It seemed highly likely. But everything seemed highly likely when it was already happening. Such as her eagerness to tear off his clothing and make love to him on the beach.

Well, why not? This was why he kept a condom in his wallet, after all.

She was an animal. He felt himself dissolving into the sand, sinking atom by atom into a singular orb of pleasure. Skyscraper lights spun like fireworks. Dock pilings collapsed and crashed into the bay. She towered above him, monstrous, ravenous, terrifying.

He didn't want her to stop.

The precarious brick buildings of Pioneer Square crumbled into the water.

She didn't stop.

A tsunami swept them up in its icy grasp.

She still didn't stop.

He didn't care if the world was ending. Stars exploded. Fire rained down. He hadn't realized how tall she was. She carried him like a baby and for one brief moment he felt safe. Then she dropped him into the churning sea. Darkness swallowed him whole.

He was not at all surprised to discover that hell was a City Target store, and that he himself had shrunk by several sizes. He must have been the subject of an alien experiment, or maybe there was something nuclear in the water. Or maybe this was karmic punishment for being a selfish prick all his life.

It made sense. He bought himself a presentable shirt and slacks from the children's department and caught the next bus home.

On the beach, the woman shook the sand out of her dress and tied plastic bags on her feet for shoes. She bought a chocolate sheet cake at the 24-hour QFC and ate the whole thing while sitting at the light rail station. The piped red icing spelled *Astonishment*.

MACH 3

At the funeral, she opened a can of fruit cocktail that was big as a can of paint. Bigger, actually. The can opener was old and got stuck every few inches. The man who had died was a farmer who shared his crops to feed the community and so everyone loved him. The funeral was more like a party than anything.

Outside by the three tall oaks, the Druids beat their drums. A woman in a toga shot arrows at a man with deer antlers on his head. Children played in the yellow mud of the abandoned gold mine. The librarian twirled her mustache and told people to read all the books she hated. *War and Peace*, *The Great Gatsby*, *To Kill a Mockingbird*. Secretly, she loved bodice-ripping romances and would sneak one home every night in her bra between her G-cup boobs. She was that alive with loneliness.

After the funeral, there was an air show. A black fighter jet flew low over the airfield. A little boy watched, mouth open in wonder. An old man told him that the plane had dropped bombs on al-Gaddafi before the boy was born.

The boy wrinkled his forehead. "How do *you* know how old I am?"

The old man was amused, but he didn't want the boy to think he was laughing at him, so he didn't laugh. He told the boy how fast the plane could fly (2,100 miles an hour). He told the boy al-Gaddafi was a dictator and that's why we dropped bombs on his country. He told the boy he'd been a flying ace during the Korean War, which was close enough to the truth. He told the boy he was proud to serve his country.

The boy couldn't take his eyes off the plane.

When he was younger, the boy's grandfather had died. The boy hadn't understood. He wanted to see his grandfather's body lying still in the coffin with tastefully painted lips, the coffin a burnished red wood that looked like a pirate's treasure chest. He was convinced his grandfather was preparing for a long voyage to a new house, perhaps sailing in a ship to an island, or rocketing into space to live on the moon. He hadn't understood the finality of death.

As the fighter jet flew sleek and low, he felt that now he knew what death was.

The woman at the funeral couldn't believe how many people had eaten the fruit cocktail. One hundred and six ounces gone, just like that. People spooned extra syrup from the crystal bowl onto their plates, licking their fingers. She herself didn't like the stuff, didn't like the chalky squeak of the grapes or the overly sweetened cherries that hurt her teeth. She wanted to eat the bitter bark off trees, suck on crabapples, crush tart huckleberries between the roof of her mouth and her tongue. She went outside and grabbed a Druid by the scruff of the neck and made him feed her green sorrel by the creek. She was that mad with hunger.

Evening fell, and three deer came down to the creek to drink. Five coyotes rose out of the darkness and nipped at their heels. The deer fled. The coyotes chased. The moon ran with them.

TALON

She crunched hot buttered popcorn in the hard wooden seat as the lights went down. The curtain rolled up, electric motor whirring. The audience gasped. A clear glass tank of blood stood in the center of the stage.

It was her period blood, gallons and gallons of it, all the blood she'd ever menstruated. The sign on the tank said it outright: *Emma Huhta's Menstrual Blood*. A magician put a giant magnet on the side of the tank and it stayed there. That's how much iron was in it. They wrapped the magician in chains, attached padlocks, put the keys in a box under the stage. They put the magician in the tank of period blood. He sank like a cannonball.

The audience cheered.

Emma walked out. She gave her popcorn to a man who called her a bitch because she didn't have a dollar. Orange syringe caps sprinkled the harbor steps. Two off-duty drag queens smoked on a park bench, wigs and heels piled between them. A busker played guitar and sang Alice in Chains covers, and fat tourists from the cruise ships lined up outside the piroshky shop.

Behind the market, Emma watched a wolf drop a kitten at the feet of a little girl. The kitten was injured and mewed piteously. The little girl called for help, but only Emma heard.

Tears stung Emma's eyes. The kitten's neck was twisted around completely. Its head and legs were limp. It cried in terror and pain.

"I'm so sorry," Emma told the little girl, "but all we can do now is end its suffering."

Weeping, the girl nodded. Emma picked up a sharp-edged shovel and slammed the blade down on the kitten's neck. It screamed louder. Emma was only making it worse.

No, no, no. Please get it right. She squared her shoulders, lifted the shovel, and brought the pointed tip down hard.

Emma and the girl were both crying as hard as the kitten now. But no one was coming to help them. Emma had to finish this herself.

Wham. Wham. Wham. The wolf-dog looked on with interest. Finally, the kitten gasped and lay still, its bloodied mouth and smashed skull a tiny stain on the earth. It was just a baby. The horror of its death should have stopped the world, but not a soul noticed.

Emma dug a small hole in the sod and scooped the kitten's remains into it. Piled the dirt back on and pounded it flat.

The ferry horn sounded and Emma couldn't miss the boat. The wolf approached with yet another kitten in its mouth, and the little girl took the shovel from Emma and told her to go.

On the boat, a woman in a polka dot dress nursed a brown slug the size of a baby. Its black knobbed antennae stretched luxuriously as it sucked. The woman stroked the spot between its antennae and called it her darling.

A middle-aged man in a Hawaiian shirt stumbled as the boat moved and spilled beer on her darling. The slug-baby convulsed and shriveled up in the woman's arms. She screamed and called the man a murderer. A federal agent came and zip tied the woman's hands behind her back. He told her it would be better for everyone if she let him dispose of the body now.

Emma couldn't hear the answer because the agent had duct taped the woman's mouth. But the agent nodded solemnly, wrapped the desiccated slug-baby in its green and yellow blanket, and tossed the whole thing overboard while the mother watched. The mother shrank then, too, shriveled up into a wrinkled hag. Her teeth dropped out as the man in the Hawaiian shirt poked her.

"You see," he said, with an ugly grin, "this is what happens when you break the law."

Emma looked out the window. The ferry was about to crash right into the mountain. "The captain's had a heart attack," someone shouted. No one could seem to find the lifeboats.

Emma put on a life vest and stood outside on the deck. If she was going to die, she wanted to die with the sun on her face.

But a cold shadow swept over her, and something like knives speared her shoulders and chest. She levitated off the deck, carried higher and higher by a great brown eagle, its wings and talons so strong she couldn't break free.

Slowly, the ferry crumpled into the mountain far below. She heard faint screams beneath her own screams. The talons hurt her so deeply they tickled her bones, and she laughed and cried in waves. Snot dried on her upper lip as they flew.

Finally, the eagle dropped her into a nest at the top of a tall fir. The nest was full of eaglets and smelled like rotten meat and bird shit. She was exhausted, but each time she fell asleep, an eaglet tried to peck out an eye or bite off a finger. So she threw the eaglets out of the nest one by one until only the runt was left.

When the eagle returned with a fish, they shared it. The sun went down. The stars rolled up. The tree swayed.

SNARE

The boy walked alone along the edge of a cliff. Below, the blue ocean rolled, bluer than the sky. He had a fishing pole and a net. He cast out the line. It snagged in a cloud and he soared, netting swallows, pigeons, and gulls.

The gulls he threw back. They were scavengers.

A tunnel in the sky spiraled open before him. He stepped in, his feet ringing the surface like a bell. The walls were white but the way was dark. Air roared in his ears like a windstorm.

He was afraid.

The tunnel narrowed and he made to go back but he couldn't see the way out. The birds struggled in his net, clawed feet and hearts kicking. A blackboard appeared, covered in chalk, strange symbols and letters that eluded him. He felt that this was who he was, somehow. A mystery of arithmetic, written in inscrutable vowels.

A furry puppet with ping pong balls for eyes asked him who his father was. He didn't know. He realized he had never known. He panicked.

There was a clown with a red wig whose fat belly strained at the buttons of his shirt. The boy wondered what else was behind the costume. This also made him afraid, but he couldn't run. He was paralyzed where he stood.

The clown popped like a balloon. Red curls went everywhere. The spiral tunnel tightened, sucking the boy in, yanking his guts in sharp circles like the teacup ride at the fair.

The birds were torn from their net. They pecked him and scratched his scalp. How could he tell them he'd only done this because he was hungry?

At the end of the tunnel, everything stopped. There was nowhere else to go. The birds were gone. He was alone. In the dark, his finger throbbed.

His fishhook was embedded in his finger. Each time he touched it, it made him cry. But the longer it stayed in, the harder it would be to take out.

With a mighty shout, he yanked the fishhook out. The pain was so bright it made him see stars. He could feel his heartbeat like a drum in his fingertip, feel the hot blood spilling out.

With his other hand, he took up the hook and scratched at the tunnel wall. He scraped away for forty days and forty nights.

When a hole finally opened, a seagull brought him a grape leaf. He ate it and was strengthened. He pounded his fists around the hole and soon the whole wall cracked and fell away.

He was on top of the clouds. There was nothing between him and the moon. He missed his home, but the pull of his heart was stronger.

He cast out his line and hooked a crater on the moon. Up he flew toward those vast gray seas.

STRIPPED

While he was sweeping the break room floor, his fairy godfather appeared.

"Tut tut!" he said, long whiskers flowing. "You're missing the ball."

This wasn't news to him. He'd always been bad at sports.

"I'm not interested," he said. He scooped up a pile of dust bunnies tangled in human hair like strange electrons. "Excuse me."

The fairy godfather refused to move. "I'm not leaving until we get you to the club. The richest, most powerful women in all the land will be there." He helped himself to a skin croissant from the box on the counter and bit into it. It was flaky and airy and crackled like bacon. Little bits of baked human skin clung to his beard. "Mmm, buttery."

"Those aren't for you, you know."

"Like your boss will miss *one*." The fairy godfather licked his fingers. "Come on. I've got the perfect tux for you."

"I told you, I'm not interested." He still had twenty-four break rooms to clean, and forty-eight all-gender restrooms. He got paid to clean offices for a law firm, not to go clubbing. He was tired of the implication that he had to marry up in order to succeed in life. First of all, he wasn't even sure he liked women. And also, what was wrong with being a janitor?

The fairy godfather took the hint and hauled off to the club by himself. He got mixed up with an Armenian heiress who caught him philandering with a cute pixie and that was that. He was ruined professionally.

A year later he showed up on the janitor's doorstep.

"No thanks," the janitor said, and slammed the door in his face.

"Who was that?" someone else called out. The door opened again. It was the janitor's boyfriend, Paul. Paul let the fairy godfather in and fed him pages from old books wrapped in prosciutto. The janitor clenched his teeth but said nothing. Soon the couple had a new roommate. Things went downhill from there.

Paul and the fairy godfather got along famously. They both loved colonial furniture and miniature topiaries. The janitor, on the other hand, missed out on their home decorating ventures because he was busy scrubbing unmentionable stains off toilets. He came home too exhausted to enjoy their gourmet meals and chic window treatments.

One day Paul announced that he was moving to Costa Rica to find himself. The fairy godfather felt bad for the janitor and stuck around for a while to help with the rent, but one day he was gone, too.

The janitor stood in his kitchen scrubbing burnt egg out of a skillet. His nailbeds were cracked and the water stung. The trunk had broken off Paul's miniature elephant topiary. There was a damn blue jay squawking right outside the window and it wouldn't shut up. His sinuses were clogged and his mouth tasted like a retirement home. He shouldn't have eaten those croissants. They were just packing on the pounds.

He sold everything he had and moved onto a llama farm. He found out he was allergic to their wool, so he moved across the road into a Buddhist temple. But eating vegan made him anemic, so he got his bartender's license. Working at the law firm had put him in constant contact with alcoholics, so he figured he had plenty of experience.

At the bar he met a rich businesswoman who liked his signature passionfruit martinis. He let her buy him dinner and before he knew it he had a red BMW, a platinum engagement ring, and a beach house with a swimming pool on a Mediterranean island. He worked on his tan all day and worked on his back all night. He felt appreciated until he had to sign the prenup.

He called it off.

Desperate for a job, he ended up at the croissant factory. Every day he watched the headless bodies swinging from hooks, passing through disinfectant showers, their purple veins an atlas of untraveled highways mapped on skin. Somewhere inside the machine, their skin was stripped off in sheets and air-dried. Their flesh was salted and cured and sent elsewhere to be made into prosciutto.

At the end of the line, the croissant skins unrolled like paper. They were smothered in butter and layered with air, transformed into delectable sustenance. No life was ever wasted.

SPIT

Everyone these days was eating sand, as much as they could find. They rolled it into marbles on their tongues. When they lapped at each other's necks, they drooled glass. It captured the sun like a polished apple.

The baker couldn't sell marble pies. She had tried, but people were still eating gluten-free. It made her laugh, all the labels proclaiming items gluten-free, even the labels on things that would never contain gluten in the first place: popcorn, salsa, canned tuna, pickled bees. It was one big marketing ploy.

She wished she was better at coming up with her own marketing ploys. The bakery was almost always empty, except for the insurance adjuster. And she came only for the cheap coffee with unlimited refills, occupying a table for hours at a time while using the free wi-fi from the laundromat next door.

Sometimes the baker thought about cancelling the free refill policy, but if the insurance adjuster didn't come anymore, she'd just end up throwing out the leftover coffee anyway. So the baker let her stay. They only spoke during their transactions, spending the rest of the time in companionable silence, watching couples eat sand on the beach outside the window.

It was as good a time as any to experiment. The baker rolled a mound of dough into a circle. She piled fresh blueberries in the center, topping them with sharp cheese and shredded basil. Rolled up the edges and brushed the crust with beaten robin's egg.

She baked the tart, then offered to share it with the insurance adjuster.

The women sat across the table from each other. Between them, slices of tart steamed on white plates. Forks grinned. The women stirred cream and stevia into their cups. The insurance adjuster asked how business was. The baker replied, same as always.

An empty bird's nest curled in the corner of the window ledge in front of their table. They watched as a joyful couple galloped up from the beach and coughed perfectly spherical marbles into the nest. Their saliva dried in silken strands as they sprinted away.

I don't suppose many people appreciate this kind of food anymore, the insurance adjuster said.

They don't, the baker agreed. She was determined not to feel her own sadness.

Well, I think it's delicious. The insurance adjuster tried to pick up her crumbs by pressing them into the tines of her fork. She gave up and blotted them with a wet finger instead.

The baker licked blueberry juice off her fork and smiled. She was remembering her former life as a Sherpa, how the pack ponies would lick the salt from her palm with their clean pink tongues. How she could breathe in the cold Himalayan air, gulp it alive, and still feel dizzy with all that height. Her blood knew how close she was to the sky.

TREPANATION

When he cried, out came everything he'd ever loved. A king of diamonds, a Parcheesi set, an atlas of world maps. A Tiffany lamp from his grandma's piano. A fork with a handle shaped like a branch. A goldfish named Nimoy and his first computer, a TI-99/4A. An Iggy Pop poster and a soccer ball. The pocket watch his ex-wife gave him on their anniversary, the one with the foxes on the case. That one hurt most of all.

Since he was already crying, he let himself cry some more. When the pile of things he loved grew so tall he couldn't see out, he climbed to the top.

From there, he could see the firmament.

The firmament looked like a fuzzy cloud. He'd never quite been able to imagine a firmament. That explained why this one was so vague.

He stuck his hand into the lavender cloud.

"Ouch!" the firmament yelped.

He apologized profusely. He was horrified, but also fascinated. He wanted to poke the firmament, stretch it thin, squeeze it into a ball. He wanted to see if it would bleed.

On the other side of the apartment wall, the wife lay on her back with her knees in the air as her husband made love to her. A thin ring of sunlight haloed the ceiling, a ring without a planet.

The ring on her finger was hot and itchy. The pills had made her gain weight. She ran her hands across her husband's chest, stretched up to kiss his lips. She was a moon untethered and hurled into space. The glass of water on the windowsill broadcast the light from the sun. The ring of light on the ceiling was like a trepanation. Any minute now the ceiling would be sawn off and the room would pop like a boil, pus and tenderness everywhere.

The husband's morning was perfect. Before waking, he'd dreamed of his college days when he was in his prime. He had showered and drunk coffee and read the news. He was going to the golf course later, and right now he was giving his wife a morning screw. Life was good.

Somewhere, a television nagged. Outside, children screeched. There was a smell of old bacon grease. The bedframe squeaked, or maybe it was a mouse giving birth in the wall. It was a difficult labor. The doctor said it had to be now. Enhance your vitality with these natural supplements.

The doctor ate a sandwich. The doctor put on gloves. The doctor caught the babies like footballs, hiked them to the nurse, carved their bits until they were perfect, went home for an afternoon screw.

The day stretched like hot taffy. It was covered in flies.

He took the firmament to the park and tore it up like cotton candy. He wasn't crying anymore. He put the firmament in a traffic cone and carried it like a torch. Its failure to cry disappointed him. But he himself was a disappointment, and so he understood.

He fed the firmament to a cluster of pigeons by the lake. One by one their bellies exploded. Bird seed and firmament everywhere. He picked up the fluff, picked up the feathers. They were purple and green in the sun. He made them into wings. But it was useless. He couldn't fly.

He popped his neck, felt a tingle in his foot. Let himself cry. This time, he cried out all the things that had hurt him. They were the same as the things he loved.

A doctor in a pink shirt walked by on his way to the golf course. He carried a bag of clubs. He smiled. He whistled. He looked forward to his beer.

His wife lay in bed, feeling like the top of her head had come off. The ring of light expanded. It grew and widened, eventually fading away.

AXE

The world was a terra cotta pot. It broke open on the head of the Universal Gerbil, which didn't care for such things one bit. It pooped in indignation, leaving five oval pellets in the blue core of the Messier 66 galaxy.

    Astrophysicists were baffled. Their broken world should have transformed, change into something else entirely. But it was they who transformed instead.

    They manifested as oil paintings of English cottages, toaster ovens, and Bonsai trees. They became in appearance like baleen whales, dark-eyed juncos, and flour weevils. The laws of the universe became more visible to them in these forms, meaning they now saw that what resembled law was really only an average of random tendencies and was subject to change over time. Which itself wasn't linear, therefore the laws could change at any moment and transform them into another existence without warning. Meanwhile, entire star systems died and were reborn, grew up and took their first steps around galaxies inadvertently created by an astrophysicist named Llew every time he sneezed.

    In one of Llew's galaxies there lived an entity named Rahm. Rahm remembered everything he'd ever learned. The size and shape of all the atomic particles. The equinoxes of each planet and the temperatures of the stars. The number of life forms in the universe. Every war, murder, and plague. Each birth, death, and transfer of organic matter between worlds (which happens more often than you think).

Rahm brewed strong tea in demitasse cups and drank it unsweetened on his balcony, watching the gaseous surface of his home planet swirl below, varicolored as a peacock's feathers.

His wife emerged from the kitchen with an axe, chopping the heads off geraniums. Her eyes were bloodshot and bulging. He wanted to hide, but there was nowhere to go except down into the gas and that would kill him. Nowhere was safe from her sharp-edged axe. She honed it every day on the tusks of imported busk minks, whose meat was the most revered and reviled in the galaxy.

Rahm was appalled on a daily basis. (This tends to happen when you're the sort of being that remembers everything.) Rahm remembered how his wife had laid a dozen red eggs in a nest of spent tea leaves and made him sit there for a month to incubate them. As soon as they hatched, she'd swallowed them whole. He had promised to purchase busk mink for her if she would stop eating their offspring. She had agreed, mocking his manhood all the while.

As he kept a healthy distance between his body and her axe, he told himself he was lucky to be married at all. The nose of the astrophysicist that had sneezed him out was particularly hairy, so Rahm had inherited unappealing Neanderthal looks. And even though the larger part of his mind was supposed to be a blank slate, ready to accept loads of new data, he felt as if he knew too much already. He had no space to think thoughts of his own because he could never forget. All he did was wait and spin uselessly until someone wanted to access his memories, and few did. It was a cruel task, this life.

Rahm blew his nose thoughtfully, admiring the green slime. He wiped the snot on his wife's mink sandwich when she wasn't looking. It was highly gratifying.

Waking early, Rahm pulled back the covers on yet another day. His wife snored next to him, smelling of garlic and halitosis. He remembered her eating the snot sandwich and stifled a giggle. If he was quiet, he could enjoy his morning tea in peace.

As luck would have it, the leaf blowers kicked on in the Milky Way galaxy, shattering his quietude and his wife's revolting dreams. "There oughta be a law," he muttered, and then remembered that laws were really just an average of random tendencies. He gave up and jumped off his balcony into the poisonous gasses.

His wife promptly forgot him. She busied herself with shouting out each line in a prehistoric COBOL manual, then pulled out her anal teeth and scrubbed them. She scoured her axe until it bled, then hacked up the African violets. She kneaded a batch of toe fungus cheese, registered as a political candidate, and made an omelet. Then she went to what remained of the broken Earth and decapitated the operators of the leaf blowers.

She came back with a new set of windchimes, positively raging with joy.

Meanwhile, Rahm took advantage of his disintegration by dissolving into a million tiny pieces and riding the wind into the exosphere.

Eventually, he drifted into space as cosmic dust. Rahm diffused himself across the universe, sailing on solar winds, sprinkling his molecules on random planets like cinnamon.

In a painting of a white house in the Scottish Highlands, Llew the physicist inhaled, breathing deeply during his Zen meditation. As a dust mote, Rahm traveled up Llew's right nostril, dodging a jungle of hairs and lodging himself in the medial temporal lobe of Llew's brain.

Llew's eyes popped open. "Crap," he said. "I almost forgot." He scribbled himself a note to buy eggs.

Deep in the folds of Llew's warm brain, the speck that was Rahm felt appreciated at last.

QUARK

The movers were tired. They had been lifting stuff for hours: up, down, sideways, minding ceilings, minding doors. Spiral staircases in both directions, one with gravity, one without. Their positrons were positively spinning. Even their lunch breaks were in question; you couldn't eat a matter sandwich here without accidentally sending some part of yourself into the abyss. Symmetric annihilation was that swift and that certain. They were lucky enough to have been born aberrations; pushing your chances any farther was just asking for it.

Besides, it wasn't a bad life, just work, followed by pub, followed by sleep, followed by work again. It could be worse. You could be the barkeep, for instance.

The barkeep had a body that was all curves. It arced and bent and redistributed light. Her body had chitinous wings, antennae, and a glorious beard, long as that of Michelangelo's God. She was on her feet all day and never slept as far as anyone could tell. She was prone to quivering fits that came on like earthquakes. She ate pickled eggs from the jar on the counter, green brine streaking her beard as her mandibles chewed. Customers yelled at her, catcalled, and never tipped.

The movers felt sorry for her, but they never got tipped either, so they drank their booze and left her alone.

One night, they noticed her antennae were missing. She couldn't hear them. They wrote their orders on a napkin and tried not to stare. The barkeep's beard was getting longer. She was out of pickled eggs. She collapsed all of a sudden and laid five dozen eggs of her own. There was no one to fertilize them, so they would rot away in the corner by the jukebox, slimy and cold.

Such a waste, the movers said, but no one was volunteering to fertilize that clutch. After some futile kicking, the barkeep managed to roll herself upright again. She wordlessly poured their ales and brought them to the table. She looked the same as always, awe-inspiring and awful, as if the lack of love and sleep she'd endured all her life had shaped her into an indomitable machine. She didn't seem to need anyone's help.

The barkeep panted as she polished the pub's displays of medieval armor with a rag. The armor had openings in the front so the males who wore them could piss, or procreate, who knew. She wasn't familiar with the genitalia of this species. But she was certainly familiar with their stench, their odoriferous pores and glands that blew a rancid stink across the pub day and night. She thought she might be sick again, but it was probably just the next clutch of eggs coalescing. Her cycle was off these days due to poor nutrition.

She stroked her beard and belched, barely dodging an errant dart. It was karaoke night and that meant lots of cocktails to mix for the men who were trying to impress their dates. Fortunately, her antennae had been lopped off when she stood up too fast under the crossed swords hanging over the beer taps, so she wouldn't be able to hear their cringey come-ons.

She felt at peace in a way she hadn't felt in a long time. She used all four arms to chop the limes and lemons, spearing garnishes of olives and onions and cherries. Her feet were killing her, but her body was electric. She was expanding like the sun. Her beard spread its fronds, infused with static. She brushed it on everyone she served.

With the beard, she could feel what each patron felt. The beard would brush against a bottle blonde in cowboy boots and, *whoosh*, the ache of loneliness would sweep right in. Or the beard would ruffle the shoulder of a man whose mustache curled over his lips, and the barkeep would be overcome by a longing for trophy bucks and guns.

She knew the movers felt pity and disgust for her, which was why she sighed with feeling whenever she served them. There had to be a sympathy tip somewhere in those denim pockets, or a hand job if nothing else. She was a perennial optimist.

Because of the beard, she knew that optimists in pubs were a rare breed, limited mostly to young schmucks whose greatest goal in life was to get laid. She knew that folks with less money were happier than folks with more money, and the folks in the middle were just happy to get by. Depression wore a push-up bra, sleep deprivation wore muddy boots, clinical alcoholics disappeared under baseball caps, and despair wore a gold-plated Rolex without fail.

The sensation of all these feelings thrilled her. Her patrons might not meet her eyes because of the beard, but it didn't matter. She knew all their secrets. She could see their deepest selves.

As the nights passed and the barkeep's eggs decayed by the jukebox, the movers asked themselves why they kept coming here. It was filthy and depressing, and if the barkeep couldn't even run a mop over the bathroom floor, it was only a matter of time until a free electron or two slipped into their beers. They could be neutralized, canceled out, and then where would they be?

As he said this, one of the movers felt something tickle his lip. He peered into his Sam Adams and plucked out a long silver hair.

To his horror, the hair was still attached to the chin of the barkeep who hovered nearby, her triple stomachs jiggling below her thorax, her wideset eyes leering.

She felt his jolt of fear.

"This is it, boys," the mover said, dropping a twenty on the table. "I'm outta here."

He winked out of existence, leaving behind an empty black hole.

"C'est la vie," the barkeep said, and chugged what was left of his beer.

EBB

Ophelia was walking along the beach when up rolled one of those glass fishing floats from Japan. It was round and green, as full of potential as an unmapped globe.

She held it up to the sunlight. Panting within was a slender, big-eyed frog.

She couldn't leave it in there. She smashed the float open with a rock. The glass cracked like an egg and the frog jumped out and turned into a prince.

The prince was an asshole. He told everyone he met that the government was run by lizards, then he accused his new acquaintances of being lizards themselves. He held doors open for people, only to let the door slam on them when they were halfway through. He told a young boy on a skateboard that his mother hated him. He tripped a portly woman in front of the saltwater taffy shop. He didn't tip the wait staff at the fish and chips joint and he held up the line at the ice cream parlor as he sampled each of sixty-four different flavors then didn't buy a thing.

He said Jake the Alligator Man was a fraud. He filmed a porno in the parking lot of the World Kite Museum. He didn't bring reusable bags to the grocery store and he licked sunscreen off women's shoulders as they walked by. The prince was the worst person Ophelia had ever met, and he followed her everywhere.

One day while she was trying to take a shit in peace for the love of God she told him to leave her alone.

He left. He found the skater boy and threw a quarter at him.

The boy pocketed the quarter and rubbed his forehead where the change had left a welt. He was used to mean people on account of living where he did. He was also used to getting hurt on account of owning a skateboard. All things considered, having an extra quarter for the peep-show machine at Marsh's was good luck. He'd take it.

As he skated away from the quarter-throwing asshole, he flipped him the bird.

"Your mother tosses salads for a living!" the prince yelled.

It was true. The boy's mother worked at the café down the street. She opened big plastic bags of premade soup into soup tureens and warmed up broccoli cheddar and clam chowder for hungry tourists. She opened big plastic bags of shredded lettuce and tossed them with shredded carrots and cabbage for the salad bar. She sliced thick whole wheat bread and smeared it with aioli to make sandwiches so tall people couldn't wrap their mouths around them. Best of all, she got to take the leftovers home.

Her son hated clam chowder but ate everything else. Some days in the winter when the days were short and her hours were cut back, his mother would worry about how to pay the rent, but they always had food.

She hadn't planned on staying in this town so long. It was just the way things went. First the pregnancy, then the divorce, then her mom's kidneys. When things got to be too much, she would visit the wise elk cow who lived at the edge of the bog. She was going there now.

The elk kept a meticulous house. Shining pots and pans with coppery bottoms hung from the kitchen ceiling, and a Roomba gobbled up stray ashes and splinters from the hearth. Pickled green beans with red peppers stood in jars on the pantry shelves, and the skulls of small animals gleamed among the dustless bookcases and webless windowsills. The elk believed in honoring the blessed dead, which was why her husband's antlers were mounted above their bed, may he rest in peace.

The elk poured her a cup of pine needle tea. They sat in front of the living room window and gazed out at the gray sky and the gray fog. The fire barked. The Roomba whined. The elk had been baking bread and the whole house smelled of goodness.

When she was here, the woman never thought about her cold studio apartment or her son's latest skateboarding injury. She didn't think about premixed soup or the dark Doug firs, so hungry in the crowded fog, closing in like bad dreams. The elk let her brush her fur, and as the Roomba grumbled at their feet, the woman recited her fears. They popped out of her mouth like raisins, the bitter gritty ones that no one likes to eat.

The elk nodded and the Roomba ate the raisins, only complaining once.

When the elk's fur shone and the woman's fears were all gone, she walked back to her apartment. Night had fallen and the wind brought rain. She was wet and cold but she was used to it.

When she got home, she stood in her damp socks at the stove to heat up some minestrone soup. Her son gave her a quarter to help pay the rent. When he hugged her, she let herself cry.

Meanwhile, the prince had returned to Ophelia's doorstep. He was drenched to the bone and shivering. He wanted her to let him in. He said I'm sorry, and, I didn't mean it, and, you're so cold.

Ophelia felt clearheaded now that she'd emptied her bowels and drunk some aquavit. She could taste the dill in her mouth. It gave her courage. She was going to put him in his place after all this time.

She opened the door and kissed him in the rain. As she kissed him, he shrank. When he shrank small enough, she trapped him in an old peanut butter jar and screwed on the lid. He skittered around like a spider as she hurled him into the sea.

SHARD

The women sucked on bits of glass for nourishment. Starlings yelled from the cherry trees that yielded no cherries. They wanted the shiny things for themselves.

When the women blew their noses, their tissues were black. They bore babies with broccoli heads and strawberry eyes. They had worked in the fields too long while pregnant, but somebody had to pay the bills. Somebody had to pay the blues. The reds were all taken. They were put to work in the radium mines. That's what they got for being traitors.

There was no one left but the yellows. The yellows knew how to starve. They were good at losing teeth and not losing their cool. They were what the textbooks called *resilient*, which was a fancy way of saying *expendable*.

Water was blue, except when it was red. Sometimes the river roared down the waterfalls like blood. Other times it was sluggish and yellow with mud. Come to think of it, they had never seen blue water. But they knew it must exist. The number of its name could not be discerned. They had seen it on the screens in their dreams. Blue water was a living thing encoded into their ancestral memories. It could not be denied.

The women sucked bits of glass to force their mouths to make water. They carried burdens on their backs and in the winter when the fields lay fallow they walked into the city. Each building there was a spire, a point made to the sky, another dot in the matrix of the landscape. Green water came from the fountains. The elevators hoovered them up like messages in vacuum tubes. There were vast wooden doors as wide as the walls. The women sucked their glass and scanned their retinas. The doors unfolded like flowers.

Inside, there were offices with king-size mattresses. Tangles of white sheets. Vending machines with nothing to eat. Toilets that knew when you got up and used the green water to flush. Windows that showed you whatever you wanted to see: snowy fields, cherry blossoms, the moon.

Everything had to be cleaned. The people who lived in the city were carriers. So the women sprayed everything with liquid that killed what the city folks carried. They washed the sheets and made the beds. They drank the green water because it was safe. They drank so much they felt drunk, dizzy with altitude and water weight.

They stumbled across cobblestones singing. The late ferry waited in the harbor to take them home. It was cold and slickly raining yellow rain. They sucked the glass so hard it cut their gums, dripped blood when they smiled. The taste of water only made them crave more. They lay down on their backs in the rain and stuck out their tongues. Drops ran cold down their lips, hot down their throats. The ferry blasted its foghorn and the city folks had to step around them but they didn't care. The water was so good they missed the boat. They slept in alcoves wet with desire, murmuring the numbers of their names. Their blue-veined flesh in the open air, ribs popping at the seams.

In the spire, it was morning. A city woman made her bed. The cleaners never did it right; she liked sharp corners and crisp pleats. She scanned her face at the vending machine, bought a carton of sanitized air. She drank it at her desk, at the window, staring out at the blue blue water rushing over rocky cliffs, at a place that didn't exist.

SIMULATION, PART 1

The simulation was complete. She rolled the smooth papyrus around on her tongue. It tasted of cave dust and spores.

Thus activated, she marched up the steps and into the light. Somewhere, a child was crying. It was the famine that had been simulated for the age to come. Starvation was necessary for the species' evolution. Without hunger, there could be no change.

The scroll in her mouth contained the algorithms for life. It was a secret only she could bear.

She squinted in the bright sunlight. It was the hottest part of the day. Of the year. Salamanders cowered in the cool of her shadow. Sand clung to the toes of her boots, sought entry through her nostrils. Her eyes stung. If she had been a different kind of being, she would have shed tears.

The tree of life drooped, wilted, in the middle of the desert. Abandoned by its guardian angels, it no longer bore fruit. It was good for nothing now but to be chopped up and thrown into the fire.

She put her back into the axe swing, used her body as the force. Chop. Chop. Chop. It was a good word for the sound. If there had been mountains nearby, her axe would have echoed until it rained, but the earth was flat as a snake's tit and dry as the surface of Mars.

In another life, she had been an arborist, climbing limbs and revving chain saws until her biceps vibrated. Skin browned unevenly by the sun, boots spiked with steel. She cut around birds' nests, tenderly, a mother protecting her brood. She ate fried hashbrowns for breakfast, lunch, and dinner and woke with the sun. She had a different bandanna for every day of the week, safety sunglasses, and a subscription to Beer of the Month club. Her life then was simple and sweet.

But that was before the simulation. Before human beings created the substance that could not die, before they remade themselves by slowly ingesting their own microparticles, before they fed the same stuff to the rivers and oysters, the birds and whales, who ate the substance that was eternal but did not grant them eternal life. A third of the fish died, and a third of the birds fell out of the sky.

Eventually, a third of the humans died. Then three hundred reindeer were killed in a series of lightning strikes in a remote pasture in Finland. It was how things went. Chemists consumed their own creations, which was either cannibalism or incest when you thought about it. Lightning sometimes struck the same place twice.

The tree of life was now a cord of firewood, neatly stacked and waiting for its afterlife. The humans laid their firstborns on similar pyres, once upon a time. A sacrifice to fire, which they knew would someday consume them all. Even before the simulation, they could sense its ultimate story, their terrible end. It was how things went.

SIMULATION, PART 2

When the simulation was complete, the singer lost her voice. After a performance, her alto register disappeared completely. It was like trying to move an amputated limb. The comfortable rumble between her vocal cords and her vagus nerve was completely gone.

A permanent chill crept up her spine and clung to her neck like someone else's baby. Everything she said came out a croak. People mistook her for a lifelong smoker, assumed she had throat cancer. It was a mystery, the doctors said. Speech therapists threw up their hands. The singer gave up her career, which was the same thing as giving up her dreams.

It is a dangerous thing to make one's living by following one's dreams. After the simulation, no one did that anymore. They kept their dreams precious and separate, crystal orchids under glass. The singer worked hard at things she did not love: kneading bread, paying bills, mending yoga pants, filtering spreadsheets. For her own safety, she stopped pursuing music entirely.

One day, her friend the inventor gave her a musical instrument that she could play with her diaphragm, bypassing the need for vocal cords. It was strapped to her chest over her heart. She could create the music by controlling her breathing.

The first few tries, she passed out. When she learned to stop herself from entering the quantum realm, she could inhale and exhale something approximating music. It sounded like bagpipes crossed with a cello, or an oboe with panpipes. She played notes she had never heard before, tunes that didn't exist. The scales had fallen away from her ears because now she could play with her heart.

The simulation didn't like her songs because it could not classify them. Her music was a threat. But it couldn't destroy her, so it made her life miserable instead.

The grocery store stopped carrying her favorite hot sauce. Her bank account was emptied. She got a weird rash on her back that wouldn't go away. Someone dented her car and didn't leave a note. On a walk, she was attacked by nesting crows. Then one morning, she woke up and her house was gone. So was everything in it.

She was lying on bare earth in her flannel pajamas with the instrument strapped around her chest. It squeezed tighter and tighter. She couldn't breathe. She couldn't get it off. She was dissolving into the quantum realm again. She couldn't control it.

The breath left her body and so did she. Everything was gray. The waves of air, the waves of water and space. She could see herself from the outside of her skin; that's how she knew she was no longer on earth. She could see the shape of her body as memory. Felt a timeless calm consume her lingering pain.

The instrument remained.

A being made of digital bits fizzed into her plane. It crackled and snowed like an ancient TV. It produced a stack of firewood and built a roaring fire.

The smoke made her lazy. She wanted to drift like a log on the ocean. She thought about the tree that made the firewood. It was alive, once, and so was she. What a mystery it was, that life!

The fire popped and warbled. She felt a pang in her sternum. The being hummed tender and dark. Her ribs buzzed in response. The hum sustained and crescendoed until she could bear it no longer. Out popped her heart like a cork from her chest.

She gasped like a diver coming up for air, her throat full and crowded with all the things she wanted to be. She grasped for her slippery heart and screamed and screamed and she was back on earth beneath the green trees in the silence, she was singing and the echo sustained her, made her blood beat, gave her back to life. She could sing again and she did not know how. But she would never again doubt her dreams.

In the quantum realm, the digital being picked up the instrument. It buckled the straps over its heart. It played then, a sweet, sad song. The simulation would have to press restart.

WHOLE

One, two, three. The cards of her life flipped over before her. Death, The Devil, The World. Tell me something I don't know, she thought. The tarot reader had raggedy ears and a lip with a fat red scab on it. She had a sharp overbite with fangs that glinted gold when she smiled.

The tarot reader was smiling now. It made her uncomfortable. She tossed over a miniature dog biscuit and the tarot reader swallowed it whole. She could see the outline of the bone as it slid down her throat, a slow-moving submarine under the skin.

She got up and left.

She walked out through the screen door. The little wires cut her into a million pieces. Each piece showed something she had done.

After forty years, it was a lot. A dollar dropped in a busker's hat. A door held open for a woman in a wheelchair. A mural painted over graffiti. Cherries plucked ripe from the tree and sold by the pint. Countless pieces of staring at screens. A teapot shattered on the floor.

But the worst pieces were the ones she noticed most. A little boy crying, blood trickling from his nose. A hamster, stiff and cold next to an empty food bowl. Drunk and shouting at her mother. Running over the neighbor's mailbox and driving away.

She had never felt so ashamed. She couldn't let anyone see her like that. She had to pick up the pieces of herself right now.

But the wind picked up and blew her pieces all around the world. Her pieces rained like ashes on the markets of Bangalore, gathered in the dusty corners of the Kremlin. She drifted into piles of rotting logs in Olympic rain forests, settled on the slopes of the Arenal Volcano. She was pollen, she was dust. She was everywhere and nowhere, and depending on who saw what part of her, she was revered, reviled, or ignored. Mostly she was observed and then forgotten. Somehow, that was worse than outright hatred.

Then a man found her. Inside him was a boy who worshipped film directors and dinosaurs. This is what made him different from other men: he found a piece of her that was teetering on an aphelandra leaf, on a plant that grew in a ceramic pot in a Canadian mall. It was the piece of her that ate an entire pot of spaghetti, then puked it back up. He was so impressed by this that he devoted his life to finding the rest of her.

It took him many years. He sailed every sea, walked every continent. Every time he found a piece of her, he watched it with the utmost tenderness.

Some pieces of her broke his heart. Others made him laugh. As he collected her pieces in a chocolate tin, he fell deeply in love.

When he was old and silver-eyed, he found the very last piece of her on an ice shelf in Antarctica. His breath quivering in the frigid air, he held her up to the dying light.

In this piece, she was a child in her mother's garden, swinging a broom to knock the dust motes out of the air. Her mother had tied pink ribbons in her hair. The sunlight gilded a lilac tree. A lonely blue jay screamed. It was the golden summertime of dreams.

The old boy's heart tugged right out of him and soared into that scene.

The girl felt a sudden heat in her chest, right where her heart beat. It was warmer than the sun. She could smell the ripening blackberries, the green of the swelling peas. She was so happy, her eyes stung with tears.

She was alone, but not alone. A strange and wonderful thing.

Then her mother called—lunch was a tuna sandwich—and the girl came back to her body. The broom dropped. The pine trees sang. The sun shone on and on.

SNAP

She was waiting at the airport when a thumb-sucking stranger climbed into her lap. He was far too old to be doing such things but she felt bad for him and didn't ask him to move. She had been a big sister once and didn't mind the weight of foreign bodies on her plump ribs and fat thighs. If it brought him comfort, he could sit there. Until it was time to board the plane, anyway.

He wore a crushed velvet shirt with ruffled sleeves. His eyes gazed at the flat nothing of Texas out the window, as empty of thought as a baby. When she asked him where he was going, he turned into a frog and leaped away down Concourse B. There was a fountain at the end full of pennies that ought to keep him entertained.

She needed a drink.

At the wine bar, beautiful women popped out of oysters and rubbed themselves on a wet hippo. They fed the hippo lotus leaves. A glass blower shaped orbs in a kiln on the hippo's back.

The glass blower lived in a retired oil derrick on a fiery sea. It was the only known sea of fire in the world and as such was a closely guarded secret. Being so close to the fire he needed for his work, he practiced every day, and quickly became a master.

Being a master made him lonely.

Earlier and elsewhere, a grandmother shelled peas on her porch. She was older than the worldwide wars. It seemed to her that she had been shelling peas forever, shelling peas since before she was in her mother's womb, since before the universe began.

She looked at the soles of her granddaughter's feet and said she needed better arch support. Then she told the story of Jack and the Beanstalk, although halfway through she suspected her granddaughter already knew the story and was listening only to humor her.

Out in the garden, a fine specimen of a man uncurled himself from the dirt. Pea vines popped and zucchini stalks bent to make way for his arrival.

He stood and rubbed the dirt off his muscular body so he could see with more eyes. The eyes on his chest opened wide. The eyes on his ribs opened wide. The eyes between his shoulder blades squinted in the sunlight. He tore the roots from his toes and walked out of the garden into the street.

The grandmother and granddaughter saw him go, but didn't find him worth mentioning.

The man's eyes let him see everything at once. He felt that all of space and time curved around him, as if he were some being from a higher dimension. The lesser beings shopped for their groceries and mowed their lawns and gossiped with the hair stylist. But he had no need of these things, because instead of two eyes, he had thirty. He beheld the higher truths. He had no need of comforting lies.

When the train came through town, he hopped on the caboose and watched the world flow by. When his eyes looked up, he saw a man in a ten-gallon hat smiling down at him. "What'd you do, rob a bank?" the man asked.

He didn't have the power of speech, so he couldn't reply. But he knew he didn't like the man in the hat, didn't like the way he was sitting above him, legs dangling loose and carefree. He swung himself up to the roof of the caboose and that's when he saw the man in the hat was blind.

He laughed and laughed and took the blind man's wallet.

Still smiling, the blind man stabbed him with a fork and put out his eye. Although he still had twenty-nine eyes left, losing the one hurt like a mother. He shoved the blind man down onto the tracks. The train wheels sprayed him into blood confetti.

The hot sun made the rest of his eyes hurt, so he closed them and fell asleep. When the train stopped, he woke up, but he couldn't open his eyes. New roots sprouted out of the places where his eyes had been. He yanked one out experimentally. There, he'd lost another eye.

Now he was both blind and mute, in a strange city with no guide. He heard distant train whistles, a man hawking papers, a seagull's mews. He smelled fried potatoes and spicy frankfurters. His stomach sucked itself inward, searching for food.

Fortunately, he was still a fine specimen of a man. A woman touched his skin and asked him if he needed some company. Flattered, he nodded. She took him into a public restroom and had him do things to her with his roots. His lack of sight made her feel guilty, so she gave him money instead of asking for any. Then she put him on the light rail to the airport. There, he spent twenty dollars on a glass of Bordeaux at the wine bar, waiting for a flight to anywhere to come up with empty seats.

On his flight, the glass blower sat between a blind-mute man and a woman with hips like Nash 600 fenders. He'd seen both of them at the wine bar during his performance. The woman seemed embarrassed that their thighs were touching beneath the armrest, so the glass blower focused his conversation on the handsome blind-mute man in the window seat. He asked lots of questions and the mute man would either nod or shake his head, so in this manner he gathered that the man wanted to come work for the glass blower on his oil derrick by the fiery sea. The glass blower thought he might finally have someone to watch Law & Order with.

The turbulence was getting worse. Her bra was biting into her back. She needed another drink. She didn't care how much it cost. It was going on the company card anyway. Her knees were tense from trying not to rub hips with the glass blower in the next seat. At least he wasn't talking to her. For that, she was grateful.

The plane shuddered. Nervous, she stamped her feet. The glass blower kept talking to the gorgeous mute man as if nothing had happened. She knew she should be used to flying by now, but turbulence still freaked her out. She punched the call button. She heard a ding and then the plane nosedived. Oxygen masks slapped out. Her stomach hurled itself toward her feet but got stuck behind her bladder.

A woman with big hair and a bigger Bible jumped out of her seat. "Believe and be saved!" she shrieked. Her husband tore open the emergency exit door and out they were sucked.

She held on to her seat for dear life as the open door sucked her toward it, too. The glass blower tried to hold her back but it wasn't working. Her seat belt strained and snapped. Out she went like a vacuumed-up crumb.

Everything was cold and white and she passed out.

The glass blower had a good grip on the woman's feet, and the blind-mute man wrapped sinewy arms around him. The woman had fainted, but the wind caught her curves like a kite, and she billowed above them like a zeppelin. Her glorious thighs had saved them.

The three of them splashed into the ocean off the coast of a green-treed island. In the water, the woman came to. They swam to shore. They were the only survivors.

They saw no other humans, only monkeys and seabirds. They were hungry, but they didn't know what was safe to eat. They tried to catch fish. It didn't go well.

The glass blower was good at building fires, so at least they stayed warm at night. The woman was lonely and wanted to mate, but the glass blower didn't like women that way. One night by the fire, she curled around the blind-mute man instead.

He felt the woman's warm thighs cup his own. He remembered what it was like to have sight. He wanted to see her teardrop breasts and the wedge of her sex. See her two eyes shining in the firelight.

He let himself be loved. He even liked it for a while. He felt the hot suck and hard gasp of her pleasure. But under the pressure of her something gave, and although she came he could not, and when she slunk away disappointed, all he could see were the red chunks of the blind man he'd thrown under the train.

In the morning, the woman and the glass blower found the blind-mute man had rolled into the fire while he slept. He was crisp-skinned and soft, and thoroughly baked.

Can you blame them? They ate and ate.

Earlier and elsewhere, the grandmother and the granddaughter watched the plane crash on the evening news. They buttered their peas and said nothing.

GALILEO

It used to be, a planet could sneak up on you like a heart attack. You could be all minding your own business, hanging out with your girl under the bright and predictable stars, when someone would hand you a tube with a bit of polished glass in it and bang, zoom! There would be a whole new world out there, easy as an apple falling from a tree. Full and ripe like it had been there waiting for you all this time.

There were speculations. Like, were those moons, or rings? Animals, or vegetables? Unicorns or angels? Were there women on other worlds? There were definitely demons. This had long been established.

The earth girls fluttered their fans in vain when the scientists discovered telescopes. They stared at the sky for so long it was all they could see. As a result of this farsightedness, the women married merchants instead, and scientists became a rare and misunderstood breed, living with their sisters who cooked and cleaned and charted the planets' courses. The women did everything while the men wrote books.

As a result of not knowing how to do anything, the men made a lot of errors in their books. Science is still trying to catch up today.

The men told stories of alien beings, creatures like and unlike us who breathed the rarified air of Mars and Uranus. Hot air balloons were built, flying machines designed, towers raised. Anything to get us closer to the planets that we loved, to those green-skinned ladies the scientists craved.

Captain Kirk was Galileo was a magus. Did you know? It's why Elon Musk shot a car into space. There's a space girl out there for every one of us. We haven't seen them yet, but we have faith. We just need to build a telescope powerful enough, strong enough to see past the stars until we finally find what we're looking for: us, inverted, alien but wise, seen through a glass darkly from the other side.

STORM

Logs fell from the sky, hard as diamonds. The time of great wind was here. It blew fire into forests, turned trees into ashes. Most people stayed indoors and tried not to breathe too deep.

The librarian stayed home. Her shift was canceled. She usually passed the time with dental floss, strangling squirrels in her backyard. She would skin them and make squirrel stew. Librarians' salaries didn't go very far these days.

But today she needed to get her steps in. So she put on a gas mask and went out into the storm with her iron umbrella. Logs bounced off it like toddlers on a trampoline. She was invincible.

At the pond, she pulled a fork out of her coat and stabbed a fat koi. It would make some fine sushi. She wrapped it in a plastic bag and put it in her pocket.

But the koi would not die. It had taught itself to breathe air a long time ago. Despite its stab wounds, it gulped what little oxygen was left in the plastic bag.

The koi needed more air, so it pushed its head out of the bag and toward the light, gills fluttering, smoky air filling its pharynx. It looked around at the world outside the librarian's pocket. It was higher than it had ever been, even higher than the time it jumped over a lily pad to catch a crunchy damselfly.

Despite its situation, the koi was in a state of awe. Three college girls braved the log storm on their roof, feinting at the sky with chairs and doors. Logs crashed into cars and clunked down chimneys. An elderly man wore a shopping basket like a helmet, trudging home with his daily groceries.

Shit, the koi thought. It took a deep breath, reminding itself it had already accomplished one impossible thing. What was one more?

The koi decided to swim through the air.

The librarian felt her pocket grow lighter. A doe and two fawns grazed by a drainage ditch, nibbling on hazelnuts. The koi swam through the air between them, smoke billowing in its wake. Blood dripped from its side into the empty ditch. The ditch bubbled and overflowed, gushing a river of blood past the deer into the street. The librarian had to jump to avoid getting her feet wet.

The blood kept coming, filling the street, washing logs down to the harbor. The librarian's white shoes were turning rust-pink.

The deer could swim, but the librarian could not. Now the blood came up to her neck. She threw her arms around the doe and held on.

The doe and her fawns were swimming with the flow, down the road toward the Sound. Covered in blood, they smelled like fresh meat.

Carnivores swam behind the deer: wolf and bear, coyote and dog. Orca ahead, cougar crouching in the trees above. They would eat the librarian, too, if she smelled good enough. She would make a fine steak tartare.

She sheltered the deer with her iron umbrella as logs plooshed into the blood all around them. They were washed out into the Sound.

A man fired a gun from the deck of his boat. He was high and hadn't slept in three days. He sensed the end of the world was coming and he wouldn't be saved.

Two kayakers had been drinking rum at the yacht club. They saw the red running into the harbor and wanted to see it up close. They floated their kayaks against the rising tide when one of them got sucked under and didn't come back up.

The surviving kayaker beached on a massive rock as gunshots rang out. An eagle circled overhead. The blood in the water rose, staining barnacles. The kayaker opened his flask and poured one out for his friend.

The librarian's arms were tired, but terror kept her clinging to the doe. They were in deep water now, the blood and the fawns and the predators swimming close behind. An orca surfaced and spouted a few yards away. Beyond the orca was a sizeable rock, and the doe was swimming toward it. She just had to hold on a while longer.

Then a small plane tore down from the sky, badly damaged by the logstorm. It plunged into the bloody Sound, sent shock waves over the librarian's head. She lost her grip on the deer, on everything. She tasted copper and raw beef.

When the world returned, she was barely breathing, coughing and choking and clean. She was on a rock next to a kayak. Her rescuer gave her a flask.

She drank, felt the liquid burn. Her umbrella was lost to the deeps. The plane was shattered. The animals gone, as if they were never there, erased by the fey and feral sea.

SCALPEL

They came for the wombs with scalpels. They said they were *protecting the land*. They wanted a future without certain children in it: the poor, the foreign, the tan. They wanted to stop the refugees and the nations that first lived on the land.

They were living on stolen land. They flew hovercars and put eyes in every doorbell. They judged you by the color of your skin and the contents of your fridge. They liked *law and order*. They liked to lick it off a spoon.

They liked money. They liked to sell people for profit. They found a way to do it without the people knowing they were sold. They made lots of money.

They cut down forests. They didn't grow them back. They ate steaks. They drank wine. They fed the tan children tacos, cheap ones made of sand. They forced them into *education*. They made them work the land.

The children grew up and the ones with wombs were scalpeled. They grew food but they couldn't afford to eat it. They tore strips off their skin and fried them for breakfast, boiled and ate their hair. When they grew old, they carried candies in their pockets. These they could suck without teeth.

The scalpeled wombs were *sterilized*, except for the ones who escaped. Those wombs staged an uprising. Uteruses Unite! They armed themselves with guns and crowbars. They beat down iron gates. They sent anthrax in the mail. They set fire to the mansions of the great.

Didn't we kill you? the womb cutters said. Don't you know your place?

The people with intact wombs didn't comment. They felt it wasn't their place. They had pale, rich, citizen kids, the kind that were born with a voice. They saw nothing wrong with the system. Clearly, everyone had *a choice*.

HARBOR

The neighbor's damn dog was barking and it wouldn't stop. She envisioned dropkicking it into the bay, then immediately felt guilty. She wasn't that kind of person, after all.

Instead, she walked to the beach and shouted expletives over the water. The rich people in their waterfront homes would hear the f-bomb echoing over their tea. Good. They deserved it for making it so expensive to live here.

A heron took flight as she screamed. Its wings were so wide it blotted out the sun. She thought of pterodactyls. She ate some potato chips and threw the bag on the sand. She hoped some rich jerk's dog choked on it. They deserved it, after all the turds they left out here for unsuspecting soles to find.

Somewhat calmer, she trod the boardwalk to the pub.

There, a tree-boring beetle gnawed its way through the wooden bar top, which was made of a long thick plank sliced from white pine. The beetle had lost its original home when some firs were felled for a housing development. After that, it had made the long journey to the pub. Despite the frequent noise, it was a good home. The beetle wouldn't run out of food for as long as it lived. The beetle was warm. The beetle was dry. The beetle was happy.

The beetle died of advanced age.

Tracking sand into the pub, the woman sat at the bar and flicked a dead beetle onto the floor. "Give me the usual," she growled.

BURN

Waking was another forgetting, a loss of power. Things you just did, you could no longer do. Flying, for instance. Outrunning soldiers. Hacking the Pentagon from a video arcade, popping an ollie in a pizza bar.

She smashed a garlic clove with the flat of her blade. The fragrance wilted her nose hairs. She peeled the garlic, diced it, sauteed it in a pan. All she could think about was punching men in the face. Her knuckles would be torn to shreds but holy fuck it would feel so good.

The steam rose from the pan in thick clouds. She wasn't looking for anything meaningful, just the unvarnished truth, rough as a week-old bread crust, sharp as a crystal of salt. She wanted to burn.

The Devastating Rabbits of Quirk were not a band, although they did indulge in singing from time to time. They knew their kind was incapable of landing on the moon, therefore they focused their efforts on knitting mandalas and planting broods of Muscovy ducks. Snails were their preferred appetizer. The rabbits had remained unchanged for longer than most other animals had lived on earth. Thus they were immutable.

The philosopher liked to get stoned, which is probably why he ate copious amounts of cheese while gazing at the stars. But the fact of his being stoned had nothing to do with his lack of professional publications. No, this was only because his peers were all dimwits. They enjoyed tearing each other down. It was a model passion in his vocation, apparently.

All he wanted to do was graft fruit trees in his backyard and riff on Sartre. Was it too much to ask?

Every time she had asked for something, the answer had been no. The garlic smoked in her cauldron. She butchered a pound of tomatoes and scraped in their guts. Juice and skin everywhere.

She crushed oregano between her palms. The scent: a lawnmower bag exploding. A spinning blade stopped by a foot. Toes leaking into grass. Gasoline.

The engine cuts out. Silence ensues.

The Devastating Rabbits of Quirk hum in unison. They are crouching under the lilac bush. They are ogling the carrots in the garden. They are endlessly amused. The cat is afraid of them.

An order that is not order appears. It is evident, now: all logic is disarray. The philosopher is not fond of admitting this, but he does. At the grocery store, the head shop, the booksellers by the quay.

Have you heard? There is nothing sure, he says, so drink the good wine now, eat dessert first, screw your neighbor's wife. Store up your treasures in your memories, which only decay when you do. What more could you want from this life?

Sleeping was another forgetting, but the good kind. When you slept, you got your powers back. You could hold the molten core of the world in the palm of your hand and not get burned. You could feel the very stones before they were born.

You could eat the stones and gain their wisdom. Your teeth would be like iron. You could cradle a sperm whale in your arms, feel its wriggling mass, oceans of ennui. You could make love to a stranger, pretend they were royalty, then suddenly they were. You could live in a castle with aquariums the size of swimming pools, aquariums you could swim in. You could start a nuclear war with a snap of your fingers. Destroy worlds, just like that.

The dreams of the powerless are their power. She knew this without knowing that she knew it. She heard knocking. She stirred in basil, sprinkled salt.

The knocking continued. It was urgent. There was no one at the door. Her pot was boiling over, the steam acrid. She wasn't wearing a bra, but she didn't care. She flung open the French doors and pounded onto the fire escape, knife in hand.

A woodpecker, white breast speckled with black, had made two neat holes in the siding. It regarded her without fear, then flew away.

The philosopher was done telling. It had all been said before. He chose a life of hermitage, surrounded by single malt Scotch and cannabis plants. He was a model citizen.

The woman put down her knife and sat on the fire escape. The knife fell between the cracks, clattered on the rungs below, and was swiftly reclaimed by a Devastatingly Handsome Rabbit of Quirk.

The woman watched it hop, blade in mouth. The sauce boiled over in the kitchen. There was smoke, then fire. The smoke detectors went off. The building was evacuated. Fire engines appeared. The woman sat on the fire escape, lost in thought.

HONEY

Their love set the world on fire. As soon as they married, the wind and lightning came, and then the entire West Coast was burning. Smoke for days and days.

For days and days they sat inside their honeymoon suite and ate Fig Newtons. They had sex once. Watched a lot of Netflix. Looked at the brown ocean under the brown sky through their hotel room windows. Ordered pizza because they couldn't afford room service. Took photos of the Mars-red sun.

The day they were to leave, the bride woke from a terrible dream. As she looked around the room trying to remember where she was, a pile of chimney brushes threw themselves on the floor.

Her husband woke at the sound. He didn't think there was anything out of the ordinary.

Suddenly drowsy, the bride went back to sleep. She woke with a start. She had a crumpled napkin in her hand.

An empty Starbucks cup sat next to her on the hotel room nightstand. He must have brought tea, she thought. A nice gesture, except he drank it. The room was incredibly warm. She rolled over and went back to sleep.

She woke up from another horrible dream just in time to see her husband walk out of the bathroom. Deep down she knew it was him: he had his voice, he had his way of walking, he was the same build and height.

But he was wearing a black sheath dress and sporting a blonde bob. He sat down casually next to her. He had the face of a strange woman, one she'd never met before.

She said his name, reached out to touch his knee. It must be the sleep in my eyes, she thought, and looked closer.

"What?" the strange woman's face said. "It's me."

The bride's stomach dropped like a cannonball. I'm having a psychotic break, she thought.

She woke up with a stomachache, heart throbbing, still in the hotel room. Her husband snored softly by her side. Everything in the room looked normal.

She was relieved. This was the real world, after all. She wasn't crazy. She could go back to sleep.

But she couldn't. She picked up the morning paper from the floor outside their door and read it in the predawn light. *5 Million Dead in Nuclear Holocaust.*

She showed it to her husband. He shrugged. Everything here seemed okay to him, so what was she all worked up about? They ate granola bars from their suitcase, drank the hotel coffee, and checked out. The hotel clerk seemed bored.

They walked to their car. A layer of fog had replaced the earlier wildfire smoke. The ocean was gray now instead of brown. When the bride breathed, it no longer smelled like a campfire. She couldn't smell anything.

They drove home on the winding coastal highway. Hundreds of cars drove past in the opposite direction. She thought there must be something wrong. As soon as she thought it, they saw the rockslide. It blocked the entire highway.

"We'll find a way around it," her husband said. They made a U-turn and soon joined the tail end of the traffic jam. They crept slower and slower until they stopped, right by the exit for their hotel. She pulled out the newspaper to read more.

"You don't need that," her husband said. He threw the paper out the window, where it burst into flames.

He turned on the radio to listen to the ball game. There was an ad for Fox News. Their car idled aimlessly on the cracked gray highway. Miles of stopped cars lay ahead. She thought about burning flesh, about the time she nearly fainted during a blood draw, about sticking scissors in the power outlet when she was four years old. She wanted to feel the cool ocean on her feet, let the waves curl around her ankles, watch a white sunset. She was tired. She'd only been up a few hours, and spent most of that time in the car.

Their fuel was low. He pulled off the exit, filled up at the gas station. It didn't make sense to burn gas idling so they went back to the beach. She waded out in the surf. It made the tops of her feet tingle. Her ankles were covered in spots. She rinsed with her water bottle but they didn't go away.

"I told you not to go in," her husband said triumphantly. The sun was going down. The air was very cold. Traffic on the highway was still stopped.

"I don't want to sleep in the car tonight," her husband said. They went back to the hotel. The parking lot was packed. The only room left was the honeymoon suite, the one they'd just checked out of. He put it on the credit card.

When they opened the door, the smell was familiar. It made her stomach clench. They microwaved Hot Pockets from the convenience store and drank boxed wine. The rash from the water had spread up her calves. She was worried. She read on the internet that you could calm rashes with toothpaste. She fell asleep with Aquafresh and plastic bags on her feet.

She dreamed she was running from a Godzilla-sized couch. It towered over her, ready to fall. But she grew wings on her feet and got away. Soon it was nothing more than a thunder in the distance. She was running in the dark on the banks of the river, the river that ran behind her parents' house. Ashes were falling, snowing into mountains that fenced her in. She could smell a distant fire, a chemical that burned. The heat was overwhelming. She gasped and opened her eyes.

In the gray-dark hotel room she watched the body of her husband breathing. He lay on his back, face up, mouth ajar. It was his face, his mustache, his chest. But it wasn't the man she'd married at all.

SWARM

When her retina detached, her whole eye popped out too, dangling by its optic nerve. It bounced like a yo-yo as she walked. It wanted to get a good look at everything. There was flashing and blurring and sidewalks and wedding cakes. Rain got on the eyeball and everything went blue. Oh god, people were looking. She was going to pass out. It was gross and embarrassing. Would her eye go blind?

She cupped the loose eye and held it up to a shop window. She saw infinite clocks. She wondered if she could afford to go to the hospital. It didn't hurt, but she was scared. Could she ever drive again? What about her job? At least she still had one normal eye. Surely she could work with that. Wear an eye patch, change her name to Captain. Adopt a parrot, name it Smee.

She had just worked up the courage to hail a cab when the skyscraper down the block exploded. Smoke and nectarines rolled out. The sweet and scorched smell made her throat want to close. With the eye in her head, she could see people running, but they were quickly overcome by raining glass and brick. It pounded down like a tsunami.

She ran too, but she was wearing the wrong shoes for running. She slipped and flailed and fell, hands out to grab the pavement. A horde of people fleeing the collapsed building swarmed around her, over her, through her, their panic palpable as a knife stab, their feet and arms and heads trampling her spine, her skull ready to blow. Her brains would spill out like boiled noodles. She would be torn apart.

But then: a hand, lifting her up. A stranger, kindness. She would live.

She was standing again. The stranger was gone. The crowd was still running and so should she. But her eye was smashed flat, dripping nectarine juice. It was unsalvageable.

LOCK

It was August, and the house was getting smaller every day.

At first she hardly noticed. The air was thicker and the walls held heat. The couch that used to fit along the wall by the front door now blocked the doorway by half an inch. She moved the couch and forgot about it until one day the windows wouldn't open. They were stuck fast in their frames.

The desk she'd bought for work now took up half the bedroom. She had to crawl under it just to go to bed. The power outlet for her alarm clock only worked sometimes. She couldn't dry her clothes without heating up the house like a sauna. The front door was sticking now, too. She could barely open it wide enough for her grocery deliveries before it slammed shut again.

The kitchen shrank until there was barely room for her body between the stove, refrigerator, and sink. The books she had purchased to pass the time teetered in stacks all around her. Dust lingered in places she couldn't reach, erupting in clouds that gave her headaches when she squeezed by. And the summer heat made her gasp and sweat like a pig headed to the slaughterhouse.

The golden light from outside was unbearable. It was too gold, too yellow. There was something wrong with the sun. The feeling of wrongness would thrust its claws up her chest when she least expected it. She would be taking a spit bath, propped up like a tripod between the crush of toilet, tub, and sink when the feeling of wrong would burn through her and the shakes would start. She felt like she'd eaten bad sushi and nearly been murdered at the same time. She couldn't focus. Nothing tasted good. Her arms would go limp and all she could do was try to breathe.

And when the air was stale and sweltering, that felt wrong too, and the whole cycle would begin again.

She told herself she was lucky to have a home. She had shelter, after all. A place to stay safe from the things that were happening out there in the wider world. Invisible things in the outside air could kill you now. It was a fact.

Meanwhile, it was so hot inside, she was sticking to things. The refrigerator, the closet handle, the TV remote all had little pieces of her skin stuck to them. Her body dragged and drooped on the stained couch, in the kitchen that was now jampacked with recyclables that she couldn't take out to the bin, on the stairs piled high with dust bunnies and unwashed laundry. She schlepped over all of it just to feel herself moving, and she left bits of herself behind: patches of skin, clumps of hair, the odd toenail.

She was always sweating and this gave her comfort because at least her pores would be clear. She stopped wearing pants. There was no point. Sometimes she would feel the ceiling growing lower and her heart would stutter and her belly would jump. She would take a slow breath, bandage the latest patch of missing skin on her hand, and keep on.

Until she couldn't keep on anymore.

One day after a pizza delivery, she bolted the sticking door and the bolt jammed. As hard as she tried, she couldn't open the door again, and all she had to eat in the house was the pizza and a box of gummy worms. After that, she was screwed. She would be cut off from the world forever.

She pounded on the lock. Her fingers fell off, pink as earthworm bait. Sweat poured down her forehead, neck, and back, pooled on the skin beneath her breasts. She was alive with fear and fire, but it did no good. She would not escape.

Later, on her bed naked in the path of the fan, she heard a drill and a clank. The creak of the door—they must have drilled out the bolt. She heard the door scrape the couch aside.

Panic grabbed her throat and squeezed. A burglar, the virus, the smoke from dead trees, it was all inside her now, filling her lungs with concrete. She was alive and afraid of desire. She was as good as dead.

JACKED

She was on the passenger side of her car, disassembling the glovebox in the casino parking lot. Two big crows perched on the hood. It meant good luck. She needed it.

There was a leaky jar of oysters behind the glovebox that had been stinking up her car for weeks. There was also a baggie of poker chips she meant to cash in. They weren't stolen, exactly. Her late uncle had accepted them as payments for the ferret fights he hosted in the woods, which were attended primarily by casino employees, therefore she suspected the chips were hot but what did that matter? The Ferris wheel where she used to sell tickets was falling off its pier into the Sound so she was out of work and broke. Her cousins were too dumb to miss their dead dad's shit. Otherwise, they would've snagged the chips before she did. Never mind that she found the body first. She was always the responsible relative, checking up on her elders.

She'd found her uncle in the bathtub with a half-deflated sex doll between his knees, and made sure to dispose of it before his children arrived. For that, she deserved some kind of hazard pay at least.

The glovebox snapped out and the oyster jar crashed onto the pavement, exploding with an odor so foul even the crows weren't interested. But she couldn't find the chips. They must have fallen back into the engine compartment.

She was about to get out and pop the hood when a man in a white tracksuit held a gun to her face. "Shut up and give me the keys," he said.

"They're in the ignition," she said. *Dumbass*, she thought.

"Get in and shut the door!" he yelled.

He started the car and squealed out of the parking lot. He smelled like chemicals. He was probably high on meth or something.

She buckled her seat belt. The car sped onto the dark highway without headlights. The carjacker's skin was crawling in the red light from the dash. It was bubbling, alive.

She scrabbled at the door locks, but he was driving too fast for her to jump out. The speedometer wobbled near 90. Something bit her arm in the dark. It had come off the carjacker's skin. She smacked it. It splatted into a puddle of blood.

The carjacker howled like a wolf. The car engine revved and the creatures on the man's skin came for her, skittering like spiders and nipping like dogs. It was all she could do to swat them off and squish them on the floor.

The carjacker drove full throttle into a hairpin curve. Only half of him was left now, the rest a skeleton covered in the biting things. The car skidded and slid, careening for the steep cliff edge that she knew was there, so fast they would flip and roll right over the guard rail and be crushed on the boulders below.

She yanked up the emergency brake and held on for dear life. The car spun three full circles and came to rest in the center of the road.

The carjacker was dead. He hadn't been wearing his seatbelt and the creatures that ate him now splattered the windows like bird shit. She had to get these things off—they were stuck on her like ticks.

She threw open the door, threw open the trunk. Got out the gas can and poured regular unleaded over her hair, face, chest, back, arms, thighs. The biting things fell off like zapped flies.

The highway was empty. She was alone. She popped the hood and groped among the car's hot innards for the poker chips. Put them in her pocket. The gas seared her nostrils, chilled her skin. Into the night she drove.

COYOTE

Hot steering wheel, sticky under hands. Bug guts dried on windshield. Dust and mold creep under black bench seats. AM radio blinds me with sound.

My toes sweat on the gas pedal. I search for jackrabbits along the broad concrete shoulder. Straight on into rainbow sunset desert. Shape shifters, cacti tall as trees. Distant mesas and mountains, sagebrush and cities… somewhere, hours from here.

I pull on the headlights. Smell the lightning before I see it. The only thunder is the sound of the eight-cylinder combustion goblin under its metal hood, the secret cloak of my muscled steed. I turn off my phone.

The bridge ahead is closed for construction. The canyon below is deep and dark. In the fading light I see an orange sign. Detour.

I follow. The detour winds hairpins down the canyon. The air grows warmer here. I roll down the window, craving a cigarette and a slice of key lime pie.

There's an old school gas station on the right, the kind with analog pumps. Next door is a roadside café, aluminum siding and dim yellow lights.

I park and light up before I notice the stranger in red flannel.

His arms are crossed. Hips rest on the fender of a rusted Bronco. His hat hangs over his face. All I see is chin cleft and whisker shadow.

A gold tooth gleams. "Ran into the detour, did ya?"

"Yeah," I say, blowing out a stream of smoke with more force than I intend. The stranger says nothing, so I continue. "You know how long it is to Taos from here?"

The stranger laughs. He means it to be friendly, but a shiver runs down my neck like a spider dropping down the side of a bucket. "I don't go to Taos," he says. "I live here."

"All right, thanks." I stub out the half-smoked cigarette in the gravel. I go into the café and order my pie from a black-haired woman with a Harley tattoo peeking out of her cleavage.

I refuse the coffee. The pie turns to salt in my mouth and I want to vomit. I'm pretty sure my phone won't get a signal here.

I ask the waitress for directions. She shrugs.

"Follow the road."

The Bronco's gone now. I get in, turn the key. The dash lights hurt my eyes. I drive as the first fork of lightning spears the sky.

I sing along with the radio, loud. It's an old song, and I can't tell you who sang it or what year it came out but I know the chorus, and in the bridge between the last verse and final chorus a clump of sagebrush flies out in front of me. I know it's nothing to worry about, just the wind. And whipping through my hair it feels good, so I keep driving.

But a rusty Bronco parks diagonally across the highway and it's not getting out of the way.

I slam on ancient brakes, slow down enough to plant a bumper kiss on the mammoth Bronco. My knees are heavy and my legs feel shaky, but I jump out.

Inside of headlights, the man in red flannel crouches over a body. It's brown, furry. Teeth angle crookedly and blood and saliva run down its neck. Guts spill, slimy and pink, tangled like wires.

My mind is numb, but my heart is electric. Wind whips off my jacket, loosens the man's hat. He scratches behind one ear, and a wet tear stretches toward earth.

"Are you okay?" I ask. My eyes sting.

He snarls, and yips. I see blood on his chin and I run for my car where I'll be safe. But I can't drive around the Bronco, it's too big, and the ditches on each side of the highway are too deep and I get stuck. The wounded being outside barks and wails, howls and cries.

If I can get to the Bronco, maybe I can drive away. I don't think. I move. He lunges, swift, graceful, deadly. His teeth sink into my shoulder and I feel the hot rush of my blood, adrenaline panic in my chest, and all I can see is the gleam of keys hanging in the Bronco's ignition and I tear the animal off me, leap into the cab, start the engine and crush the body of the fallen coyote under its tires. The man in red flannel shrieks like a hawk, weeps like a child.

Thin spots of brown blood dot the windshield. It begins to rain.

ORBIT

The girl rode her bike in circles around the block while her mother flailed and gibbered in the grass. There was that same black beetle again, popped open like a walnut, soft white guts oozing out.

The neighbor's dog pooped on the lawn. The neighbor didn't pick it up. Mom mom *mom* the girl yelled, but no one answered. Her mother was busy flopping like a fish and couldn't be bothered. The girl rode her bike in another circle. There was that stupid gorilla birthday party again. She hated gorillas. She thought they were stupid.

The gorilla blew out its candles and ate all its cake. Its providers, two research scientists who couldn't have children of their own, clapped their hands and sang.

The gorilla knew they meant well, but this was all rather childish. It smeared a glob of frosting along its brow and considered the laws of dialectics.

Through the trees, a drone recorded the gorilla's movements. The drone operator, a teenage boy named Aidan, was supposed to be doing his algebra homework. He wanted to free the gorilla from its captivity and return it to its ancestral home in the jungle. It made him sad to see wild things locked up like that. It was why he didn't go to the zoo anymore.

At the zoo, a penguin named Ronny had just escaped. He hadn't meant to escape, exactly, but here he was, loitering at the bus stop pecking at dropped change. The only person who talked to him was a young woman with no teeth, and she kept trying to sell him some pills in a plastic bag so he got the hell out of there.

Before her addiction consumed her, the young woman had been a yoga instructor and a llama farmer. All she remembered of those days was the rank odor of wet llama wool. It would cling to your nostrils for days.

The Buddhist monk who took care of the temple across from the llama farm remembered the young woman who used to work there. She brought him fruit sometimes and left it on the porch, mostly apples but once in a while some blueberries. If he had not taken a vow of celibacy, he would have asked her out for tea. He enjoyed sitting in the tea shop and watching the world rove by. His sense of inner stillness became heightened by witnessing all that movement.

The little girl with the pink bike rode by the temple again, hair flying straight out from under her helmet. Mom mom mom *mom*, she yelled, in a way that didn't expect an answer. The monk put on his sandals and went out for a walk.

He walked to the tea shop and sat by the window with his iced black chai. A teenage boy and a gorilla sat outside, holding an intense dialogue with their hands. The monk knew just enough sign language to understand that they were discussing the problem of causal determinism.

Before he left the tea shop, he bought a scone to give to the addict who frequented the bus stop but never seemed to get on the bus. She never seemed to eat, either. There was something familiar about her, but asking questions would be selfish so he didn't do it.

He took a detour on the way home and saw two women in lab coats shouting frantically that were missing someone named Kelly.

"You mean the girl on the pink bike?" he asked. They waved him off.

Around the corner, a woman was having a seizure in her yard. Her limbs spasmed like an electrified squid. The girl on the bike came around, ringing the bell on her handlebars. A penguin ate a dead beetle off the sidewalk. *MOM*, the girl yelled.

The clouds scudded by like missiles. The monk felt utterly serene.

PLANK

The death of the matriarch came at a very bad time. But is there ever a good time for death?

She died during a plague, when funerals were banned. Her son owned a curio shop and so he kept her body in the refrigerator with the bottles of liquor and other potions until a proper service could be held.

People came to pay their respects. Soon the shop was filled with wilted flowers and melted candles. The shop was already stuffed to the gills with crystals and wooden ships in bottles and ceramic bookends depicting naked mermaids with strategically placed tails. The imported cheese and spice case was nearly buried in stacked crates of Barbados rum, and plague doctor masks adorned the Russian icons and Buddhist figurines. He believed in letting people grieve, but there was simply not enough room in the shop.

He bought a rundown boat and docked it in the harbor. He put the matriarch's body under a clear glass dome on the deck. His mother, in a see-through butter dish.

The people loved it. They brought flower garlands and teddy bears and sympathy cards. They came all hours of the day and night. Some people even slept on the boat, lovingly wiping the funeral dome clean every morning.

There was still a plague going on, so eventually visitation to the boat was banned. Then autumn came and more people died. Tourism dried up. The shop only stayed in business because of an increase in liquor sales. Then a once-in-a-century storm hit the region. The boat was torn from the dock and hurled into the ocean.

The matriarch's remains slid out of the boat in their big butter dish and sailed away.

The son was distraught. He didn't know what to do. He chartered a fishing boat and went out to sea to look for his mother's body. He saw no birds. He caught no fish. It was dark and icy cold. He wanted to give up and almost did. But then he saw his mother. She was walking on the water.

She didn't look so good. Her flesh had mostly sloughed away, revealing bones. A few gray flags of skin flapped in the wind. "Don't be afraid," she said, and he knew his mother's voice. A mighty grief rose up in him. Salt and water stung his eyes. The waves spiraled higher, lifting his mother to the sky.

"Don't go," he said.

"I am with you always," she said, and then she was gone.

The crew turned the boat toward home. The eastern sun was rising. The son heard the plague was over. The matriarch was dead.

AXIS

"Don't touch me!" he yelled. "I don't like being touched." The monster on the bus looked annoyed, but shifted its reptilian bulk so it wouldn't rub against him when the bus turned a corner. Faint bebop music whirled from the monster's earbuds, which were probably clogged up with brown ear wax. Could there be anything more disgusting? He doubted it.

The day was like an uncut cake. No one could enjoy it; it was just for show. Everyone going through the motions, pretending it was normal to paint stick figures on the walls of caves with their bodily fluids and seagull bones. If you drilled a hole in a seagull's leg bone, you could play it like a flute. That's how advanced this civilization was. A whole army of flute players, five hundred and one dead birds.

Not a chance of getting to the Couth Buzzard in time for open mic signup. The bus was stuck in traffic where it always got stuck, at the Mercer Mess. It was astonishing how much pollution people could justify in order to live in air-conditioned cubicles every weekday. He wondered what that would be like. A piece of gum was stuck to his shoe. There was something crude scratched into the Plexiglass window. The bus smelled like spoiled hamburger meat. Didn't these monsters use mouthwash?

The bus was gaining altitude. He could tell because his ears popped. Looking out the window, it seemed to him that the buildings and the freeways were sliding down, slinking beneath the earth. The dome of Saint Mark's on the hill grew larger, then disappeared. Soon all he could see was sky, gray as the back of a female gull.

The monster unwrapped a dental pick and dug at its gums.

That did it. He pulled the cord for the bus to stop. His plans were shot, anyway.

When he got out, he guessed he was a few thousand feet above the city. The air was cold and clear and smelled like ice. He took a few steps toward Green Lake, then stopped. He wasn't sure how to navigate the atmospheric plane. No matter which way he went, he couldn't seem to change his altitude.

A flock of jellyfish waddled by with matching raincoats and backpacks. A loose tentacle brushed his thigh, sending an unpleasant jolt through his bones.

"Sorry," the jellyfish mumbled.

His teeth buzzed. "I don't like to be touched!" Even here, he could get no respite. Someone was constantly up in his space. He frowned. He hoped his frown would scare people away. It took a lot of effort to keep this look on his face.

Somewhere below him, a tanker in the bay chirped its signal. It sounded like a dial-up modem. He was staring down at the nipply tops of mountains. Something in him broke open, then he knew.

He was a dandelion seed, sailing on the wind. He was a brown pelican, fierce-beaked, on the hunt. He was a man without a home, a child newly born. The world and everything in it was his spaceship, and he was the alien being. It was almost too much to bear.

RUMBLE

Honey dripped down the tree. Giraffes licked it, their rough black tongues scrubbing the bark. Bees stung their mouths but they kept going. The sweetness was there for the taking.

Below the tree in the parking lot there were two large trucks. One was taking clothing donations and the other was scanning breasts for tumors. This worked out rather well for people who didn't like wearing brassieres. They got a twofer.

The man with the breasts saw this on his walk. He'd been putting off his mammogram. But he'd been living with his breasts for a long time and felt they were probably fine. He didn't want a stranger touching them and squishing them between plate glass. Didn't want to know if cancerous calcifications were scattered in his tits like spilled salt. He would live or he would die and that would be it. Let the fates decide.

He read the news. The president had the virus now. It was only a matter of time. He ate a scone with honey, wiped his lips and went to shave. He had bought himself a nice red brassiere for his birthday. He was wearing it under his Slayer shirt.

He wasn't doing anything else for his birthday. It was just another day. The bars were all closed and there was nothing good on Netflix. He was tired of masturbating. Tired of walking around the block. Tired of buying groceries at the same store. Tired of lines at the pharmacy. Tired of sun, tired of rain, tired of smoke haze and whiskey. The car battery had died and he didn't know his neighbors well enough to ask for a jump so it was just sitting there in the garage.

He had a table saw in the garage but he hadn't used it to make anything in years. The smell of sawdust made him lonely. The squirrels squeaking in the rafters made him lonely. The barking of the neighbor's dog put him on edge.

He liked edges, though. They were places where things could be seen for what they really were. He would stand on the edge more often if he knew anyone would see him. But most people thought they'd already seen it all. They all lived in boxes. They lived their lives watching things in boxes. They thought everyone should fit in boxes.

Spear me like an olive, he thought, and drown me in vodka. It could be fun. He was wondering how to find someone who would do this for him when Kate Bush's "Cloudbusting" song came on the radio. He'd forgotten how good the song made him feel. He felt ridiculous for feeling so good. He felt a little guilty, in fact. He blamed his evangelical upbringing.

He microwaved some of the tuna casserole he'd made three days ago and ate it with all-natural ketchup. He was almost out of toilet paper. He needed to go shopping soon. But it was his birthday and he didn't want to.

Then an earthquake rumbled the floor and clinked the glassware in the cupboard. Ridiculously, he ran to steady the television in the living room. The shaking went on for what seemed like a century. Giraffes stampeded down the avenue. He could see them out his window. He felt loose and fluid. He could seep right out the door and trickle to the river, past the cannery and the docks out into the deep blue sea, his red brassiere mermaid bright.

When the shaking stopped, he was surprised to find that most of his stuff was in its place. He straightened his framed print of the surface of Mars, painted by that artist from Portland. He could neither read the signature nor remember the name.

He opened the door and went outside. Everything was fine. Birds sang and cars drove by. He began to wonder if he'd imagined it all.

Then he saw it. A long hairline crack down the middle of the road, stretching as far as he could see. Tiny black frogs swarmed out of the crack, legs jerking like spiders. The road yawned open and out came a woolly mammoth in a block of ice. The frogs licked off the ice, freeing the mammoth, which opened its ancient eyes and bellowed like a man unhinged.

Startled, the frogs scattered. They crawl-hopped onto the man's face, their sticky toes spreading microbes from the mammoth to him.

He tried not to breathe, but it was too late. An age-old virus was in his blood, self-replicating and renovating his internal organs. It acted fast. After being frozen for 20,000 years, it had to make up for lost time.

But time was never lost, only miscounted. Though it shouldn't be counted at all, he thought. It's not a finite thing.

He felt the pressure in his sinuses build, watched the mammoth stomping cars. Through the budding headache of his fever, he smelled the rising salt of the tide, and then he smelled nothing at all.

GRAVITY

It was morning but still night. Women jogged with headlamps like coal miners in yoga pants. There was fog that might be smoke. The moon had set long ago and the sun had yet to rise. The trees were ghosts of their daytime selves, dissolvable as sugar.

The unsolved puzzles of the world littered the shoulders of the road. Pieces of chain link fence, lumber scraps, plastic tampon applicators, mismatched salt and pepper shakers, a combination lock with no numbers, a safety deposit box with no key. When the sun rose, the street sweeper would take them away, but each night the mysteries returned like mushrooms after rain. After the bars closed, a singing drunkard might pick one up and quickly throw it back. Anything that raised doubts about the nature of reality was guaranteed to harsh a good buzz. And during those uncertain times, all most folks wanted was a cozy quilt of oblivion.

The next day, the drunk woke up with his hair falling out and his eyes in a bowl of clear gelatin. He peed and sipped coffee. Made a list. The list was all genders and numbers and races. The numbers might have been ages. He felt he was channeling something old and terrible, as if a bayonet might pierce him through and release the foul odors of putrefying flesh. Wonderful, awful. It was all so awe-full. The land called out to him with blood on its face. It demanded restitution. It would not be satisfied until it broke his back.

Backwards he went, his chair tipping over. Dumped into the abyss.

HARVEST

They gathered the women's hair in apple boxes. It was heavy, it was dark. It was long and glorious. The women were now bald. They were now naked. They had no homes, nowhere to go. Their spirits were crushed like grapes.

The hair traveled on to Bermuda and Japan. It went to Milwaukee and Illinois. It was bundled and braided, tied and brushed. It was silky on its newfound heads, salon chemicals burning, nostrils aflare with the knowledge of its own beauty. The hair was a thought of its own.

The hair felt anxiety upon its separation. Its identity had always been relative to the head upon which it grew. The hair was uncertain of its future. It had been uprooted and relocated without permission. It would now be sold.

It was good, strong hair. It would not break. You could bend it and twist it any way you liked. It would not complain.

At night, sometimes, it would be lonely. It might cry. If you caught the hair crying, you had to punish it to make it stop. Give it a reason for its tears. You could offset all kinds of bad habits and reward the good ones: silence, industry, obedience.

After all, the hair had already been cut. You did not need it to grow.

LEVIATHAN

They were tying his feet to the anvil. Down he looked. The anvil was gray. The zip ties cut into his ankles. His pinky toes were blue. He thought if they fell off, he wouldn't even notice. He was that far gone on whatever they'd given him.

But he could smell the water. He still had his sense of smell.

They opened the van doors. The night was dim and orange. Mosquitoes buzzed. He thought of the Moors, how they had conquered western Europe and built square castles. Four corners declaring the heavens. Then nuclear warfare, now peace. The word peace looked like a slice of pizza and he was hungry now, wasn't that odd? He couldn't even move his arms.

Drool pooled in the corners of his mouth. He swallowed, and it felt like swallowing a rock. Even the rocks at the bottom of the lake would taste better. Perhaps a newly evolved species of fish, brought up on the plastic waste diet of the Anthropocene era, would chew him out of his zip ties. He could hold his breath. He was sure of it. He'd been practicing for days now. The trick was to not black out, because when that happened, you started breathing again, and underwater that would spell death.

Oh, but he was going to die sometime anyway, and he felt strangely calm about it. There was the water, smelling strongly of fish, algae, and bog. They wheeled him out on a dolly, him and the anvil, stacked twins in a stroller. There was nothing in his pockets. They'd made sure of that.

He felt cold. That's why he had no pockets—he was in his underpants. He looked again. They weren't *his* underpants. The last time this happened had been when he'd peed himself in second grade. He'd thought he couldn't go on living after that. But here he was.

A meteor streaked whitely on the sky. Its trail hung there for some seconds before dissolving. The dolly wobbled up a gangplank onto a boat. The weight of the anvil dropped the boat down. His stomach sank to his knees.

The water lapped at the boat's hull, slick and livid as oil. A scaled beast rubbed its back along the boat and for one great shudder he thought they would all be tipped into the lake, but it was not to be.

He used to go fishing at the lake in the park as a kid. Reeling in plastic bags and old boots. One time he caught a whole foot. With a shock, he realized it was his own foot. The bone and skin gnawed on, as if worried by a dog.

A dog barked in the distance. He must have heard it before he thought of the dog. He wiggled his toes. He could feel a few of them. Oars splashed and collided. The water slapped. He snapped to attention, his neck craned like a turtle. The deep center of the lake was calling to him, calling like a gong. It was rippling with meaning.

THRUST

She was remembering, she was dreaming, she was planning. Up and over the puppies in the fenced yard, inside the musty smell of her grandmother's car, sipping on tequila from an unmade bed. Her head was heavy with her hair. She was strong. It could all fall out and they could amputate her left breast and still her eyes would see and her ears would hear and she would live.

Breathing, breathing. The stark confederation of autumn hearts. The spiders and crimson leaves, the torn grocery lists, abandoned masks, a party with a medical theme, they were all dancing in their finest frayed jeans from the year when they couldn't find flour to bake bread. They were curling up their skeletons like bedrolls, like German pastries or yoga mats. They rolled their bodies like Turkish carpets, coiled and fat.

It could be all you ever wanted, this dance: six feet apart under the open sky with the cold crows buzzing. Stinkbugs raining ballads, chewing thighs. Their jaws can cut through wire, that's how strong they are. The dogs running after tossed bones, rattling in their teeth like dice. Fates collided, hadrons numbered.

The gate of the city is sealed. No one comes or goes. The markets are empty, the rivers barren. Up grow the fish like weeds, evolving roots, evolving lungs. Pairs of everything.

The animals are winning. Back the earth, buck the skin. Bucking shorn tradition. The royal tree within. Butter up the madman, honey. The race is about to begin.

RESISTANCE

She trimmed her toenails on the closed toilet lid, not too close, just enough. There was beef jerky in the cupboard to last them a week if they were careful. No one picked up the phone anymore when she called, so there were no answers. She would have to keep chipping away at her soapstone sculpture, one wet chisel at a time.

The stone could get as slippery as ice. It was tricky to work with. One minute the slope of the shoulder would be almost perfect then the next, too much shaved off the side. She closed her eyes and felt the rocky muscles in the dark, her fingers finding truths her eyes couldn't see. There, the pimple that wouldn't go away. Here, the scab from the itch from the sport detergent that kept getting scratched off again and again. The nipple with the scar from the botched self-piercing ten years ago. The curve where the rib muscles tensed protectively over the spine, the hunched bait of electric tigers, oily as rain.

The packets flooded their protocols like grains of wild rice. They were uncooked and dry, hard as teeth. They resisted light, resisted insulin. They could shock you like sharpened claws. She was resisting arrest, resisting stasis. She had to keep moving on.

IVE

The closer you are to death, the more tender you are towards life. That's why the chemist was so loving; she boiled uranium cores all day and cradled the heads of COVID patients all night. Their lips smack-sounding of wagon ruts, dry as American dust.

The cause and the cure were the same. She couldn't blame anyone but herself. The relations between skin grafts were axes of horror, telephonic conquests that rattled the foundations of flight. You could burn your phone on an airplane and nosedive. The wings might find two rivers and the cockpit sail on to the Pentagon. A giant snaps his fingers and *krrrrrrrr,* crash, the city's collapsed. Its inhabitants spilled out like broke whiskey.

River keeps on growling. Curses slip of skin, card of box. Sanitizes vipers in the smokestacks. The array is marvelous. All those buttons and dials. Tell it to print and the machine will live. It is language that imprints on life, living that kickstarts language. Expression: fatigue. There are too many words for fear. Actions gum up intentions. There are not enough words for all the ways you can be.

STREET OF CRANES

Overnight, the leaves had turned red. She was looking out the window, adjusting her keyboard of ribs. After her shower, she carefully dried in between the black and white keys. The ivories were yellowing with age like the yellow haze in the sky, and the bellows of her lungs flip-flopped when she constrained them in her bra. But no matter. The world was older than she was, and it would keep on living for quite some time. Plus, she had at least another decade in her. Maybe two. Yes, why not two?

She dressed as a maharaja, adding a golden veil for modesty. Her arms were flutes and her legs were oboes, shiny and black as dark matter. She had conversations to interrupt and news to break over the heads of unsuspecting neighbors like cheap crockery.

But as soon as she went out, she got sidetracked. There was a dead squirrel in the hedgerow, deflated and bursting with worms. She ate the worms and the squirrel came back to life. She got nipped for her troubles.

"Typical," she said, examining the smooth round bite on her skin. It made a new hole for her flute arm and she found she could now hit that elusive high G.

A buck sidestepped into the road, three coyotes nudging his heels. He wasn't afraid, but he seemed annoyed. The coyotes were silent as fungus, branching, growing. They were a network of bulging veins.

The buck was big, but he didn't stand a chance. Soon his hooves would tangle in fur and he would fall. Buckled knees, strapped chest. Wheezing out his love. She knew this and yet did nothing. Coyotes had to eat, too.

She saw a man in a crane lifting a house. A hundred years it had been there growing moss in the dandelion lot and now it hovered noiseless in the air like a UFO. It had four walls and a roof but no floor. You could see its nakedness.

The neighbors were taking pictures to peruse in their own homes later, in the privacy of boxes with floors. A box without a bottom is merely a lid, she thought, and a bottom without a box is a serving tray.

She had a silver serving tray from her second marriage that she used to serve tea on. It was tarnished now, yellow as this infernal sky. The whole world was upside down. Nothing was where it should be. If it was true that people had an average of 60,000 thoughts per day, why was she wasting so much time on this one?

She pulled the golden scarf high over her nose and tried to breathe. She had so much to say, and no one to say it to. It was a matter of utmost importance.

BOIL

The world's most perfect lover licked her teeth. He was secretly searching for slivers of meat, leftovers of their erstwhile meal.

She shuddered because it looked to her like rows of alpine evergreens had suddenly bared their teeth. A round of hard cheddar skidded whitely on red poppy fields. She was hungry and had a stomachache at the same time.

The world's most perfect lover revealed everything at the right time. It was the time when the water pipes were green. They grew slick algae in their cores, spewing cerulean streams. On their waves bucked tiny villages, seafaring platform communities formed during the latest depression.

She felt her carelessness rise and undress. The old ways did not concern her anymore. She was a creature made new.

The small things fighting for existence on the waves wouldn't understand. Their world was their platform. They were always fighting. They could sail no place of their choosing. Everything was light. They could float away with a breath if they laughed too hard or loved too late. Purple was the ballast of their hearts.

Ballast, ballast, that wondrous stuff! It would pull you down but it would keep your boat from sinking. It would withstand water but not knees. It could light up at the snap of a finger, burst Kelvin pinwheels on your hand.

Demand. That was what the lover did. Demanded softly, demanded lightly, reprimanded his own self. Walking on toes in the water, his thighs like gravlax, pink and cold.

I begin to understand why I shouldn't write poetry, she thought, and blushed in her chest.

The bloom of tea comforted her. The people on their platforms watched the ocean boil. The world's most perfect lover licked them, searching for meat.

SWELL

She slashed the tires with her buck knife. One, two, three. Left the fourth one alone as a favor. She couldn't be 100% merciless all the time. It was exhausting. This would have to do.

She felt to make sure her mask still covered her nose. It had an annoying habit of slipping off, threatening to reveal her to the camera eyes in the parking garage and alley.

She fell down a manhole, but she wasn't a man. There had been some mistake. She couldn't climb out. She was next to an underground river that glugged like a boiling pot. She thought of frogs cooked alive, her own legs splitting like sausages.

So much for her sense of power. She put her nose to the wall, feeling for a way out. She walked on like this for some time.

A jockey rounded the corner and tried to ride her like a horse. She stabbed the jockey with her buck knife, swipe-twist. She didn't trust people she met in dark places.

The sewer went on and on with no way out. A miniature horse splashed into her path. It was sad and missing its rider. She patted it on the neck.

The horse's neck swelled up like a blister and ballooned into a second head.

The new head was human. It had a mustache and goatee. It had white needle teeth. It opened its mouth to speak.

Outside, on the surface, a girl took out the garbage. She hated the dumpster, hated the alley. It reeked of piss and cheap weed. She hated being home alone in her mother's ground floor apartment eating pizza rolls and American cheese.

As she closed the dumpster lid, a howl shook the buildings, knocking her to the ground. Car alarms squealed. Her pants were soaked from the greasy puddle she'd fallen into. She ran to the apartment but couldn't find her key. It must have fallen in the dumpster, or she'd locked herself out. Either way, she had nowhere to go for the next three hours until her mother got home.

She heard the howl again, louder this time. The earth shook, the pavement rolled. Rain poured from the sky in sheets. Night was coming and the power went out. The streetlights blinked off. She was cold. Leeches stuck to her bare feet. The price of being born female was weighing on her.

She pulled the leeches away and out gushed her blood. It was black in the dark on her blue skin. She felt like she might faint. She dropped the leeches down a sewer drain, where she heard something big gobble them up.

She jerked back from the grate. It rose up with a screech. Out crawled a lady in torn clothes and a mask. The look in her eyes was murder.

BUTTER, SHOT

The stick of butter would not soften. That's how cold it was, or at least how stubborn it was. The Nordic snowflake nightgown clung cold to her skin. The propane heater made a dramatic racket, to little effect.

It was like this in November. Everything you planned would go awry. Trips would be canceled, stores would close. Second and third scans were required. Your whole life was one big cotton swab, shoved up a sinus cavity and swished. If it came out covered in slime, you won. You got to sit at home watching butter soften for 72 hours straight.

It was excruciating, this wait. She could melt the butter and make mustard gravy but she didn't want to. She wanted something else. Something gravid, dense, and sweet. She wanted something that could break a window. Fill the hole in her heart. Build a new pyramid, brick by brick. Catalog the stars.

But here, nothing worked. The circuit breakers had all tripped out, their 20/30/40 tongues cockeyed and sure. The interrupters unlit, daring her to press their reset buttons. You could burn too hot here, they seemed to say, and turn yourself right off.

But it was too cold for that to be true. The wires and the slot-eyed gasping outlets were masks of confusion. In solitary, you could give voice to anything, even a lie.

Lies went down soft like butter. They didn't stick in your throat. Gave no indication of their toxicity. You could swallow their fat salty sweetness and never know until it was too late. Your arteries hardened. Your brain lost oxygen. You were breathing fine until you couldn't anymore. Your lungs shredded like party streamers, polluting the ocean, choking the fish. You could spread those lies all over your skin, prepare yourself for the oven. Crisp up like a roasted duck, the crackling sparking on your tongue.

The butter was sweating. The butter was sweating bullets. That's how you could tell it was caught by the truth. *Ting ting ting* the brass bullet casings hit the butter dish. It was raining cordite. It was raining lead. There would be a hammer and explosion and then the universe, positrons negating themselves with electrons, their sex creating light.

How could you argue with a weapon like this? You couldn't. Creation was destruction was creation again. Girl Scouts sold Samoa cookies. Store employees committed theft. Tech bros jumped off bridges, bounced back up again. Waitresses cracked their teeth like nutshells.

The stress was too much. There was a fissure in the emptiness between molecules. It got bigger until everyone could feel the vacuum, the nothingness sucking at their hearts like a Dirt Devil. There was today and tomorrow and the day after that and when you looked in the mirror you saw yesterday and the day before and the day before that. Forward and backward, time was the same.

But the test, though: that was something different. The test was how you marked your days. The symptoms, the appointment, the letter with results. Positive or negative. Antimatter or matter.

The antimatter people went off into a world of their own. They had to avoid annihilation. Get clearance pot roast delivered to their door. Brown the meat in butter. Take vitals. Count the reddening leaves.

The matter people had not changed, so they went on as usual. Went to church and the beach and the store. Watched butter soften for cinnamon rolls. Waited to be transformed into antimatter, waited to ascend.

ACKNOWLEDGMENTS

Thanks to Unsolicited Press for believing in this weird little book. Gratitude to the editors of *The Pitkin Review* for being the first to publish "Skydiver," and hearts & hearts & hearts to will for including "Hunt" and "Burst" in the debut issue of *Not My Style*. Love always to my family, friends, readers, and fellow writers, who keep me going.

ABOUT LIZ KELLEBREW

Liz Kellebrew is the author of *Water Signs* and *The River People* (Unsolicited Press). She received the Miracle Monocle Award for Innovative Writing, and her fiction has been shortlisted for the Calvino Prize. Her poems, essays, and short stories appear in various anthologies and journals, including The Conium Review, Room, and Under the Sun. She holds an MFA in Creative Writing from Goddard College. Learn more at lizkellebrew.com.

ABOUT UNSOLICITED PRESS

Unsolicited Press is based out of Portland, Oregon and focuses on the works of the unsung and underrepresented. As a womxn-owned small publisher that doesn't worry about profits as much as championing exceptional literature, we have the privilege of partnering with authors skirting the fringes of the lit world. We've worked with emerging and award-winning authors such as Sommer Schafer, Amy Shimshon-Santo, Brook Bhagat, Mari Matthias, and Amy Baskin. Learn more at unsolicitedpress.com. Find us on Twitter and Instagram at @UnsolicitedP.

www.ingramcontent.com/pod-product-compliance
Lightning Source LLC
LaVergne TN
LVHW040056080526
838202LV00045B/3661